THE FAKE BRIDE RESCUE

TEXAS HOTLINE SERIES, BOOK #8

JO GRAFFORD

Second Edition. This book was previously part of the Disaster City Search and Rescue Series. It has since been revised and recovered to be included in the Texas Hotline Series.

Cover Design by Jo Grafford

ISBN: 978-1-944794-69-9

GET A FREE BOOK!

Join my mailing list to be the first to know about new releases, freebies, special discounts, and Bonus Content. Plus, you get a FREE sweet romance book for signing up!

https://BookHip.com/JNNHTK

ACKNOWLEDGMENTS

Thank you so much to my wonderful beta readers, Mahasani, J. Sherlock, and Auntie Em, plus my wonderful editor, Cathleen Weaver. I also want to give a shout-out to my Cuppa Jo Readers on Facebook for reading and loving my books!

ABOUT THIS SERIES

Welcome to the Texas Hotline, a team of search and rescue experts — police officers, firefighters, expert divers, and more. In an emergency, your sweet and swoon-worthy rescuer is only a phone call away.

CHAPTER 1: RENT-A-DATE SERVICE
SERENA

The door to Serena Chandler's apartment banged open, and her roommate glided inside without bothering to shut it.

"I just returned from a lunch date at the Bisset du Jardin Cafe," Iris Fahrenbach announced, tossing her gem-studded clutch on the entry table. "When were you going to tell me they fired you?" She flipped a handful of auburn hair over her slender shoulder. The toe of one glossy, red Christian Louboutin shoe tapped an impatient cadence on the hardwood floor.

Serena bit her lower lip and pretended to study the screen of her laptop. She'd been perched on a stool at their cozy dining nook for over an hour, though she hadn't succeeded in getting more than a few sentences typed on her doctoral thesis project.

"It was more of a mutual parting of the ways," she assured, reaching for a pencil. She idly tapped the eraser against the side of her screen.

"Is that so?" Iris demanded in a disbelieving voice. "I thought you needed that job."

"I do," Serena grated out. "Or did," she amended in a milder tone. "I'll get another one."

"You mean you don't have another one lined up yet?" Her friend looked horrified.

"Whoa! What's up with all the interrogating?" Serena tossed her pencil down, folding her arms and hugging them against her chest. Though she kept her tone light, the truth was, she was afraid. Afraid of the fast-dwindling balance in her checkbook. Afraid she might not land her dream job as soon as she hoped. Afraid of being left completely alone in the world after her upcoming university graduation.

"According to Victor, you left his family's cafe over a month ago." Iris used the first two fingers on each hand to place phantom quotation marks around the word *left*, indicating she still didn't believe Serena's leaving was voluntary. "We're best friends, Serena. Roommates, for Pete's sake! We're in this together. I think I deserve to know stuff like this."

Serena shrugged. "Honestly? I planned to say something after I landed a full-time position at Star-Corp. I really didn't want you to worry between now and then." She was currently serving as one of their low-paid, online interns, though they were making noises about turning it into a full-time, salaried position after she earned her degree. That was why she was working on her dissertation in Biostatistics instead of job hunting. The sooner she secured her PhD, the sooner StarCorp would be able to offer her a contract as one of their field reps.

Iris's hazel eyes narrowed on Serena's features. "I reserve the right to worry about you as often and as much as I want. I don't need anyone's permission, least of all yours."

Serena uncrossed her arms and blew her bangs out of her eyes. "Thanks, I think."

"You're welcome." With a self-satisfied smirk, Iris spun around to shut the front door. "You'll be thanking me again, when you hear what I'm about to contribute to the cause — something that will make your life a bazillion times better."

Serena chuckled as she hooked her ankles around the edge of her stool and returned her attention to her computer screen. This was the part where her bestie would offer to lend her an ultra-expensive dress or, better yet, serve up some indulgent dessert to try to get her mind off her troubles.

"Let me guess. Ice cream makes everything better," she teased, a theory she happened to agree with wholeheartedly.

"Hardly." Iris's dark brows shot upward. "Ice

cream only makes you fat. Money is what makes everything better."

Serena stiffened, not liking the sudden brittleness of her friend's voice. "That's not true," she protested. Yes, she happened to be in desperate need of funds at the moment, but lots of things besides money made a girl happy. Hot pink nail polish, for one thing. Plus, homemade strawberry jam, kittens, and frivolous romance books to name a few other favorites.

Iris's red-painted lips flat-lined. "Are you saying you'd rather have a bowl of ice cream right now than enough money to make the car payment you have coming due next Tuesday?"

"We-e-e-ll..." Shame made Serena glance away. It was hard enough being the poor friend in their dual living arrangement, but it was even harder knowing her friend had figured out she was driving a car that wasn't paid for.

"And don't think I haven't noticed all the hot bouillon and tea you've been consuming during the past two weeks." Iris's gaze turned stormy. "You're practically starving yourself to make ends meet, which makes me feel every shade of guilty."

Serena's gaze rounded in shock. "I can't imagine why. You're in no way to blame for the rough patch I've hit." Rough patch was putting it mildly. It had taken every last cent of her savings to cover the copays for her adoptive mother's extensive medical treatments before she passed away. That, and Serena had been forced to sell their house and nearly every stick of furniture in it to pay the outstanding balance at the hospital. Then there'd been the funeral expenses. Thankfully, she was nearly finished paying those off. Yeah, things had been tough for her lately, but she harbored no regrets. The woman who'd rescued Serena from the foster care system had been worth every penny of her finest efforts.

"I feel guilty," her friend retorted, "because I don't work half as hard as you do, yet I earn more than ten times what you do."

"I don't begrudge you one drop of your success." Serena inwardly shuddered at the thought of what her friend did for a living. *No, thank you. I'll remain respectable and poor, thank you very much!*

"If you had any sense, you would."

Serena merely shook her head and offered her friend a tight smile. She braced herself for the offer her friend was about to make, fully prepared to turn her down. Again.

"I also feel helpless, because I could snap my fingers and make all your troubles go away, if only you'd let me."

"Don't." Serena held up a hand. She knew Iris was referring to her wildly successful Rent-A-Date service. It was a highly controversial topic that they'd previously come to an agreement on, and it sounded something like this — Serena wanted nothing to do with it. Though she believed her friend when she insisted she kept things classy and professional with every single one of her clients, it was a business that held zero appeal to her. She believed with all of her heart that falling in love was something that should happen naturally, not something that could be rented out, purchased, or otherwise manufactured. Love was a gift from above. Period.

"Just listen to me," her friend pleaded in low voice.

Serena shook her head, seeing no point in discussing it again. "We've had this conversation too many times already, and my answer is still no." No apologies. No arguing about it. Just no.

"This situation is different, I promise."

Serena seriously doubted it, but she watched curiously as Iris click-clacked her way across their living room in her gorgeous heels and disappeared down the hallway leading to their respective bedrooms. *Hum. Guess this conversation is over.* She'd assumed it was leading up to something she wasn't going to like, but okay. Maybe Iris had gotten a call on her business phone which always remained on vibrate. She often slipped out of the room to answer such calls privately and discreetly on the single earpod she wore.

She reappeared moments later with a silver tablet in her hand and click-clacked her way back to Serena.

Guess we're not done talking after all. Serena bit her lower lip in consternation. She watched Iris tap the screen of her tablet a few times. Then she turned it around to display a full-screen photograph.

Serena could only assume it was one of her roommate's clients. The guy staring back at her had a fresh haircut, dark tan, and aviator sunglasses hiding his eyes. His ripped forearms were crossed in a defiant gesture, and his expression was serious — more like a scowl. He certainly wasn't going out of his way to look inviting. Or datable, for that matter. For some reason, she found that thought appealing.

A chuckle escaped her. "He looks ready to hurt someone."

"Like I said, this gig is different. No public displays of affection required. In fact, he was pretty clear about the fact that he's not looking for any form of romance whatsoever. In his application, he stressed that he's an all-work-and-no-play kind of guy."

Serena seriously doubted that. "Yet he wants to rent a date, huh?" Which struck her as a little odd, considering his appearance. He certainly didn't *look* like a guy who would have trouble finding a date.

"He just needs a plus one of sorts by his side during an upcoming event. No strings attached. It's all business, my friend, something that even you can handle without compromising your standards. I promise."

No strings attached, huh? Serena chuckled again. She couldn't help it. She'd heard that line way too many times. There were always strings attached when it came to stuff like that. There just was. "Sorry. I'm still not interested in renting myself out in any shape or form. If you need to vent about this guy as a client, though, lay it on me, chickadee. I sense a story behind him, and that's what friends are for."

"Sorry to disappoint you, but there's no venting necessary this time." Iris's perfect porcelain features adopted a smug cast. "His name is Ransom Keller. He started off his career in the Special Forces, and he's currently serving as a fire rescue worker. What he's asking for is a fake bride to attend his upcoming twentieth high school reunion with him."

"A fake bride, huh? That's a thing?" Serena asked dryly. She could only assume it meant that he needed someone to pose as his Mrs.

"Yes, it's a thing," Iris retorted cheerfully, ignoring her bestie's less-than-exuberant tone. "Remember all the times we played pretend as children?"

"Um, yeah, but I distinctly recall our husbands being imaginary." Mostly princes, come to think of it, with an occasional gallant duke or rugged cowboy thrown in.

"Well, it was excellent practice for this." Iris gave an unconcerned wave. "All Mr. Keller needs is for you to slip on a wedding ring that he will provide and walk through the gym door of his alma mater at his side."

Wait. What? "Me?" She stared in alarm at her friend. "What are you talking about?" She was pretty sure she'd made it clear that she wanted nothing to do with this rent-a-date stuff.

"You and Ransom Keller are going to pretend to be a married couple — the kind who looks as comfortable together as a well-broken-in pair of shoes. And for the itty bitty inconvenience of suffering through one short weekend of married life, how does this sound?" She named a staggering sum of money.

Serena's jaw dropped. "That's an absolute fortune!" she gasped. It was more than she normally made in an entire month at the cafe. That is, before they'd let her go. She currently had no income, which was more than a little terrifying. If she didn't land that coveted job at StarCorp soon, well, things were going to get a lot worse for her.

"It's a cushy little job." Iris's hazel eyes twinkled with glee at Serena's response. "And it's all yours if you want it." She stepped closer, playfully tilting Ransom Keller's photograph from side to side a few times. "Because you desperately need the money. Because I should be allowed to help my best friend when she's in trouble. And because I adore you to the moon and back."

Serena nibbled her lower lip in agitation, hating to admit — even to herself — that she was tempted to just take the ridiculous job and kiss Iris's feet in gratitude. Maybe she could wear a wig or something to hide her identity. While her mind raced to consider every angle, a new wave of uncertainties flooded her. Along with them was one big burning question. "Why aren't you taking this job for yourself?" she demanded breathlessly. "It's a weekend. You don't have classes. Though I appreciate you wanting to help me out and all..."

Iris's expression turned innocently blank. "I'm already booked." She turned off her tablet and lowered it to her side. "So the honest-to-Nellie truth is this: You and I would be helping each other if you agree to take on this gig. Turning down good customers happens to be bad for my business."

At Serena's silence, her voice turned wheedling. "Would you rather I beg? Because I totally will, if it makes you feel any better about doing something you consider to be beneath you."

"If you're trying to guilt me into doing it, it's not working." Serena unhooked her ankles from the stool, thoroughly enjoying the way her friend's face fell.

"Because I've already made up my mind do it," she added with a long-suffering sigh.

"Seriously?" Iris's smile reappeared and blossomed to its full brilliant wattage.

"Oh, come on! I think we both know I can't afford *not* to accept any reasonable job offer at the moment." The jury was still out on whether serving as a rent-a-date qualified as a reasonable job. She reluctantly reached for Iris's electronic tablet. "May I?" She might as well drill down into the fine details of what she was getting herself into.

"Of course." Iris eagerly flipped the screen back on and handed it over.

They bent their heads together over the photograph of Ransom Keller.

"I don't consider what you do for a living to be beneath me, per se," Serena confessed in a low voice. Iris had always kept her hands clean and her clients respectable. "It's just not the way I want to meet the next guy I date, okay?" It felt too mechanical. Too calculating. Love needed more breathing room. More spontaneity.

"Which is why I don't date my clients," Iris informed her breezily. "Not normally, at any rate," she added, indicating that it wasn't entirely out of the question.

"But you have, huh?" Serena wasn't sure why it bothered her, but it did. Even live-in-the-moment, frivolous roommates like Iris Fahrenbach deserved true love.

"Would you think less of me if I admit that I have?" Iris taunted in a teasing voice.

"I don't know." The notion unleashed a whole new wave of misgivings inside Serena.

Iris adopted a thoughtful expression. "Okay, I have to know. What exactly do you find objectionable about it?"

There was nothing quite like being put on the spot. Serena found herself scrambling for the right words to make her case without hurting Iris's feelings too much. "Maybe because the process feels too much like a business transaction."

"That's exactly what it is, sweetie."

"Well, where's the romance in that?" And what about the element of Divine guidance? Because Serena definitely intended to consult the Big Guy upstairs before venturing into her next relationship. She had done a really poor job of picking the last guy, and a heart could only take so much breaking.

Iris shrugged. "I'm not asking you to date anyone. My advice is to keep it professional, collect your fee, and get back to being a grad student. But don't be surprised if you enjoy it more than waiting tables." She smirked knowingly. "Just saying."

"Whatever." Serena made a face. Yes, she needed the money — desperately — which was the only reason she was agreeing to do this. However, the only thing she was planned on enjoying was the paycheck at the end.

"While we're on the topic of romance, though, I'd like to point something out." Iris spread her hands. "At least my clients come with resumes and background checks. That's more than you got with a loser like Victor."

Ouch! "True," Serena murmured. No, she wasn't looking for romance during the fake bride gig. It was still going to feel awkward, though, to pretend to be something she wasn't. No way around it.

"I'm sorry," Iris said quickly. "I shouldn't be joking about Victor like that. It's too soon."

Serena gave a humorless laugh. "Nah, he's fair game." Her ex was like a big, ugly scab that needed to be ripped off. It was past time to stop mourning him and move on with her life. Maybe this fake bride gig had an upside, after all. If it got her mind off of Victor for a couple of days, she was going to call it a win.

She handed the electronic tablet back to Iris. "I'm just glad this guy looks nothing like him." Victor Bisset was all pressed shirts, silk handkerchiefs, and cologne; whereas Ransom Keller looked, well, the exact opposite. Rugged. Outdoorsy. A man's man.

She glanced down at her black jogging shorts and sleeveless white t-shirt. "So tell me the rules. I imagine Ransom Keller will be expecting me to show up in something other than workout gear."

"Good guess." Iris cocked her head critically at Serena. "The Camden Hall reunion starts this evening with a homecoming dance."

"This evening," Serena gasped, glancing wildly at the clock on the wall.

Iris ignored her gusty burst of panic. "We're talking cocktail dress, makeup, heels, and an up-do. Tomorrow morning is a charity run at the John Piedmont Memorial Park. Then there's a picnic brunch right afterwards. You'll need a sundress for that. Here. Follow me." She angled her head at the arched doorway leading to the hall. "I'll lend you a suitcase and help you pack."

"Pack!" Serena's panic spread from her midsection to her mouth. "What for? I guess I just assumed this job was in Dallas."

"It is," Iris assured in a smooth voice. "It's at the Rio Grande Palace. Mr. Keller indicated on his application that he reserved the penthouse suite for his lovely bride. Don't worry," she hastened to add when Serena started to splutter. "It's just for appearances. You'll have your own room. Lock. Key. The whole enchilada."

Serena wrinkled her nose, thinking back to her own high school days. *Shoot!* They'd thrown a hotdog and s'more roast for their five-year reunion and there was chatter about going inner tubing down the river for their ten-year reunion. "What kind of school holds their twentieth reunion at the Rio Grande Palace?"

"A very posh, very private, all-male, college preparatory academy."

Meaning Ransom Keller was wealthy. "You're kidding! Please say you're kidding me!" Serena hadn't yet changed out of her gym shorts, but already she was feeling out of her element — *way* out of it.

"I assure you there's nothing to worry about." Iris didn't bother looking up. She was too busy tossing clothing into the designer black and white herringbone suitcase she'd unzipped. It was resting on the white leather bench at the foot of her bed. Like the bench, the rest of her furnishings were minimalistic white and chrome. Very mod. The only splash of color in the room was her and her phenomenal wardrobe.

"But I'm not accustomed to moving in high-end circles!" Serena moaned. "You know that! I'll be bumbling all over myself, trying to remember which fork to use and—"

"Trust me. The guys will be way too busy drooling over Mr. Keller's smoking hot wife to even notice."

His fake wife, you mean. Serena's brows rose. "How old is he, anyway?" She did a quick mental calculation. A typical high-schooler was eighteen at graduation. Add twenty years to that, and...

"Thirty-seven, darling. Eleven years older than

you, which means he'll be all grown up and mature, unlike that rat-faced ex of yours."

"You might have a point." Serena leaned weakly against the doorway, watching. Her borrowed suitcase was fast filling up with items from Iris's closet, which was probably a good thing. She doubted much of anything in her own closet would be adequate to wear at the Rio Grande Palace. The only part of it she'd ever been inside was the conference center — to attend a seminar while earning her undergraduate degree. She'd not so much as entertained the thought of renting a room there. The place was so out of her price range that it was laughable.

"Go shower!" Iris glanced up from the suitcase and waved both hands in a shooing motion. "When you get back, we'll start trying on dresses." She glanced at her watch. "And make it quick. Your limo will arrive in less than two hours."

A limo? Gulping like a fish, Serena headed for her room, wondering what exactly she'd gotten herself into. Then again, she was being paid so well that it would have been ungracious to complain.

She showered as quickly as she could and returned to her bedroom, wrapped in a towel. She stopped short at the sight of Iris standing beside her bed. She was holding up two cocktail dresses.

"Well, make yourself at home, darling." Serena gave an exaggerated wave of her arms. Though neither of them was in the habit of locking their doors, there'd always been an unspoken agreement between them to knock before entering.

"Your door was open." Her friend gave the dresses an impatient shake. "Which one do you like best?" The first one was a halter-style dress with a bouncy skirt in a shade of deep royal blue. The other was a sleeveless ensemble with a high neck in a shimmering sea-green fabric that seemed to roll like water as it moved.

"No little black dress for me, eh? I thought black was slimming." Serena had already made up her mind which dress she wanted to wear, but she couldn't resist teasing Iris a little first.

"You're slim in any color," Iris shot back, "and the only place for black in September is boardrooms and funerals."

Chuckling, Serena moved toward the sea-green dress. "This one looks like an ocean wave about to crash onto the beach. What kind of fabric is it?" Whatever it was, it was beautiful,

"Good choice." Iris tossed the halter dress over the foot rail of Serena's antique oak bed. "It's made of iridescent silk chiffon, and you're going to look stunning in it, Miss Blonde and Blue."

Serena soon found herself enjoying the break from her studies more than she should have. What kind of woman didn't enjoy a good pampering session? She allowed Iris to pin up her hair and lend her a pair of diamond earrings. As she peering into the mirror she was sitting in front of, she wondered if this is what Cinderella had felt like.

"You don't, by any chance, have a pair of glass slippers hiding in your impressive collection of shoes down the hall?" She winked at her friend in the mirror.

Iris pursed her lips. "Now that you mention it, princess..." She glided from the room and returned with a pair of four-inch heels dangling from two fingers. They boasted a thin, silver base, but the pièce de résistance were the straps over the toes and around the ankles. They were nearly transparent vinyl and studded with crystals.

While Serena slid her feet into them, Iris backed up, hands resting on her hips while she surveyed her work. "For a gal who's so at home in ponytails and gym shorts, you clean up well."

"What can I say? I have a pretty amazing fairy godmother," Serena admitted ruefully.

"That you do." The smugness was back in Iris's fine-boned features. "Now go be happy for a couple of days, will ya?"

"I'll try." Serena pressed a hand to her heart. As much as she tried not to think about it, Victor's betrayal still stung. They'd been dating for over a year, and she'd been secretly browsing wedding dresses on her phone the day she'd discovered he was cheating on her.

"I mean it, Serena." Iris's tone was severe.

"Forget college, and forget your ex for a few days. You need this."

Well, I need the money, anyway. "You're right. I do." Serena took a deep breath and smoothed her hands down the lovely skirt, willing the butterflies in her stomach to pause their incessant fluttering. "I can do this," she added in a whisper.

CHAPTER 2: FAKE PROPOSAL

RANSOM

Keller.

Ransom's gaze narrowed in the mirror on the name badge pinned to his dress blues. For days, he'd been debating on whether to wear a suit versus his Army uniform to tonight's homecoming dance. In the end, his uniform had won out. This was who he really was — an ex Special Forces guy turned fire rescue worker after a major injury that had gotten him medical boarded from the Army. He considered the half crescent Special Forces badge emblazoned in bright gold letters on his shoulder to be his single biggest accomplishment.

Why try to hide it? There was certainly no hiding the limp that accompanied it. Some days it was worse than other days. Earning his badge might be his biggest accomplishment, but his limp was his biggest souvenir from his stint in the military.

It wasn't as if he had a woman in his life to impress, thanks to two demanding careers that had left so little time for dating. His high school sweetheart had turned him down flat years ago, when he'd asked her to follow the drum. He hadn't bothered proposing marriage to another woman since.

As Ransom conjured up Macy Parker's soulful blue eyes — he'd always been a sucker for big blue eyes — and pouty, kissable lips, he couldn't help wondering if she'd be present at their high school reunion. She was a social butterfly, so it wasn't too much of a stretch to imagine her dating another one of their classmates after she'd ended things with him. He just hoped it wasn't a member of the Pack. That was what he and his four closest football buddies had called themselves. Man, but they'd had a lot of fun together! Too much fun, according to their parents.

There was also the possibility that Macy Parker had done more than date another classmate. It was possible she'd gone and married one. The Pack had gone pretty quiet on him during his Special Forces years, come to think of it. He'd always wondered why. At first, he'd assumed it was because they'd started getting married, one by one, and were busy raising families. But was it more than that? Had they additionally been trying to spare his feelings?

It made him doubly glad that he'd decided to hire someone to spend the weekend posing as his wife. Sure, it was giving in to shameless pride, but there was no way he was facing his classmates without so much as a girlfriend to show for the past twenty years. Being a member of the Pack came with certain expectations in the romance department — expectations he'd sorely failed to live up to.

Fortunately, they wouldn't have to find out, thanks to the woman he was paying handsomely to pretend she gave a rip about him.

A ring of the front doorbell alerted him to the fact that his limousine driver had arrived. With a final flick of his hand through the wave of hair that persisted in curling over his forehead, he turned away from the mirror and grabbed his suitcase.

He limped his way across the great room of the Mediterranean style home he'd inherited from his parents. The rooms were painfully empty and silent these days. Once upon a time, his childhood home had been full of laughter and mischief, boys' sleepovers, and impromptu basketball games in the driveway. Now, no one but ghosts of days-gone-by roamed the hallways. He was toying with the idea of selling the place and moving somewhere that made more sense for a single guy. However, he'd not yet been able to bring himself to call a real estate agent. There were simply too many memories he wasn't ready to let go of.

With one last look around the too-big mansion, Ransom grimaced and opened the front door. He was looking forward to heading to the hotel. Even though he would be sharing the penthouse suite with a perfect stranger, at least he wouldn't be alone for the next couple of days.

"Evening, sir." The uniformed driver gave Ransom's Army uniform an appreciative nod as he reached for his suitcase. "I'm Jarvis Marks. Pleased to meet you, Sergeant Keller." He wore his white hair clipped short and smelled like he'd dipped himself in pomade.

Ransom was surprised to hear his rank correctly stated. Not too many folks were familiar with Army ranks. "Did you serve in the military, sir?"

"Sure did, soldier. I was a medic during 'Nam." Jarvis moved toward the limousine with precise, disciplined movements. He stowed Ransom's suitcase in the trunk and ambled back to the passenger side of the car.

"Thank you for your service."

"I enjoyed every minute of it. What about you? Did you get to see any action, son?" Jarvis's silvery gaze fell to Ransom's uneven gait as he held open the passenger door. "Never mind. Looks like you saw your fair share."

Ransom grimaced. "Yep. I caught a few shards from a hand grenade in Afghanistan."

"At least you lived to talk about it." Sympathy and admiration infused the older man's gaze.

Ransom nodded and took a seat, not bothering to explain that he'd thrown himself on top of an injured comrade during the explosion. Though the gesture had cost him his military career, the soldier had survived, which made the sacrifice worth it. To this day, he considered it the defining moment of his adult life.

His father and both of his grandfathers had served in the Army. He was pretty sure that serving their country was something that ran in their family's blood. Thankfully, he'd found other ways to serve since returning home to Texas. Instead of carrying a machine gun, he now welded a firehose and ax. It was every bit as exciting and dangerous. Even more importantly, it meant he was still in the business of saving lives.

Jarvis took a seat behind the steering wheel and adjusted the rearview mirror to meet Ransom's gaze. "There's a fully stocked beverage bar back there if you need to wet your whistle."

"Thanks. I'm good for now."

Jarvis made a few more adjustments on his dashboard, checked his watch, and released the emergency brake. "I take it tonight's a special night for you?"

You can say that again. Ransom nodded. "It's the opening festivities of my twentieth high school reunion."

"Nice!" Jarvis guffawed as he hit the gas pedal. The car rolled smoothly away from the curb. "That's the one where the extra weight and receding hairlines start to show. Not that you have anything to worry about in that department, son."

True. Ransom had always made a habit of avoiding fast food and convenience foods — two things that could pack weight pretty quickly on a person if they weren't careful. His thoughts turned to more morose topics. *Then again, I've never had a reason to make a quick detour through a fast food line.* He didn't have a busy wife who volunteered at a half dozen places in town, nor children in 4H clubs or on sports teams. He had absolutely no one in his life to show off or brag about, whereas most of the classmates he'd be seeing this evening did. His loneliness settled around him like a suffocating blanket.

The rest of the drive to Miss Fahrenbach's discreetly unmarked rent-a-date office passed in silence, punctuated by nothing more than a few concerned looks from Jarvis through the rearview mirror.

Ransom had memorized Iris Fahrenbach's online profile. She was a stunning redhead, a little on the thin side for his tastes. On the upside, she was a twenty-six-year-old doctoral student. A theater major, to be more precise, which meant she was both creative and smart. It was entirely possible that her rent-a-date service was some sort of theatrical experiment or even a dissertation project, come to think of it. It really didn't matter so long as she lived up to her reputation.

He'd joined an online chat group of business executives to scope out her service, wanting to make sure he wasn't getting himself into something ill-advised. However, she'd proven to have a solid reputation for providing strictly professional dates for rent. Nothing on the shabbier edges of the law.

On the phone, Miss Fahrenbach had additionally assured him that she spoke three languages and could carry herself with ease in a great number of settings — from formal gatherings to boardrooms to business conferences. He could only hope she could just as skillfully dial it back a notch and play the part of a doting bride at his upcoming class reunion.

As Jarvis nosed the black limousine into the parking lot of a ritzy looking high-rise business complex, Ransom couldn't help being impressed with the location. It certainly lived up to her reputation as a successful entrepreneur.

Right as Jarvis brought the vehicle to a halt, a slender blonde stepped from the building. A doorman followed, carrying her suitcase. Ransom frowned thoughtfully at the lovely creature. She was wearing a stunning high-necked blue-green dress that shimmered as she walked. In the next moment, he suffered a stab of disappointment at the realization that she didn't possess Iris Fahrenbach's red hair. And who could blame him? What were the odds of running into a second woman with a suitcase at this exact building at this exact time of day?

Apparently little to none, since the woman walked straight up to his limousine.

No way! His heart pounded in anticipation. Though his contract with Iris Fahrenbach stated she was allowed to substitute a coworker under certain conditions, he was surprised she was doing so without first informing him. Then again, maybe she'd experienced some sort of personal emergency. That would certainly explain a last-minute change of plans. He hoped she was alright. Regardless, he wasn't complaining about her choice of substitutes.

Jarvis leaped from the driver's seat to open Ransom's door. He stepped out and faced the woman, inclining his head respectfully. "Clearly, you're not Miss Fahrenbach."

"No. I'm her best friend, Serena Chandler." She gave him a nervous smile and scanned his features with wide, worried eyes. Blue ones — the kind that started off with a sucker punch to the gut and worked their way to a resounding heart twist.

So much for his plans to have only professional thoughts about his fake bride this weekend! "I hope she's well?"

"She is. She's simply overbooked, so I'm helping her out for the weekend." Serena bit her lower lip. "That is, if it's okay with you. If it's not, you're welcome to cancel and receive a full refund, no questions asked."

Yeah, that's not happening. Despite his irritation

over not being given a heads-up about the switch, Ransom couldn't come up with a single objection to the stunning blonde standing in front of him. She looked classy and feminine in a sparkly sea-blue cocktail dress. And petite. Even in her heels, she was a couple inches shorter than him. She was a little nervous around him, too, which made her come across as all the more genuine. Her shy, unpracticed smile made it unlikely that she was a theater major like Miss Fahrenbach, and her deer-in-the-headlights expression suggested she was unaccustomed to helping out with her friend's Rent-A-Date business — something his friends would most likely misinterpret as nervousness about meeting them for the first time. All in all, she presented a believable picture. No, it was more than that. She was absolutely perfect for the role he needed her to play.

He held out a hand to her. "Nice to meet you, Mrs. Keller."

She gave a soft chuckle and shook his hand, looking relieved. "Thank you for being so understanding about the last-minute switch."

His upper lip curled incredulously, and he found himself reluctant to let her hand go, though he did. "Only a complete idiot would object to spending a few days with someone as lovely as you."

Confusion briefly flashed across her fine-boned features and was gone. Or sadness. Or maybe it was a bit of both. "Thank you," she murmured.

Jarvis, who'd been glancing in puzzlement between the two of them, hurried forward to grab her suitcase from the doorman. He stowed it in the back of the vehicle. When he reached for the passenger door, however, Ransom waved him away, preferring to be the one to hold it open for his very beautiful, albeit very temporary, Mrs. Keller.

Jarvis waited until Serena was seated. Then he brushed past Ransom on his way to the driver's side of the car. "Lucky dog," he muttered.

Ransom couldn't have agreed more. Inside his head, he was grinning from ear to ear. Though he was trying his best to keep things light and casual between him and Serena Chandler, his gut was telling him he'd stumbled across someone really special in her. He could already sense the graciousness in her, and the kindness. It was his tremendous fortune that she'd decided to help out her friend this weekend, as opposed to next weekend or the weekend after that. Feeling more than a little awed over the slim odds of them meeting like this, he took the seat across from her and shut the door.

He caught Jarvis's gaze in the mirror. "If you'll give us our privacy, please." Though he knew the guy was dying to eavesdrop, Ransom needed to square away the details of his arrangement with his fake bride before they reached the hotel.

"Of course, sir." Jarvis looked mildly disappointed as he rolled the glass window shut between the front seat and the main cabin. A set of louvered blinds encased inside the glass soon made him disappear from view entirely.

Serena fiddled with a silver beaded handbag. "It would probably be best if I confess something right up front."

Ransom studied her in fascination. "Oh? What's that?"

"I've never done anything like this before."

He wasn't the least bit surprised. It was kind of obvious with the way she was acting. "Neither have I."

"Really?" Her eyes widened in amazement, drenching him with more of that gorgeous blue.

"Really. And since you're being so transparent about stuff, I'll do the same. Hiring you is more about saving my pride than anything else. Couldn't stand the idea of attending my high school reunion alone, while everyone else shows off their wedding pictures and kid pictures."

"Why?" She shot him a curious smile. "Don't get me wrong. I'm grateful for extra income this weekend, but there's no shame in being single."

Again, he was struck by the sadness that wafted across her classical features. He sensed a story there. Her statement about needing the income puzzled him, though. She didn't exactly look hard up for money. Because of his affluent upbringing, he recognized things like designer shoes and well-tailored clothing.

"Huh!" he snorted. "Wait until you meet the Pack."

At her blank look, he explained. "Five football buddies and all of them rabid jokesters."

"Nice!"

"Far from it, I'm afraid. To say they had high expectations of me in the romance department is putting it mildly. They'll never let me live it down if they find out I don't have so much as a girlfriend to show for the past twenty years of my life."

Her smile widened. "Seems to me that the sixth member of the Pack might be the biggest jokester of all."

He quirked an eyebrow at her. "How so?" It was true. He couldn't deny the fact that he and his friends had been locked in an unending battle for years to one-up each other. Which made him all the more anxious to hear her thoughts on the topic.

"You acquired a wife. That takes leg pulling to a whole new level."

"Thank you."

"Wow! You're actually proud of it."

"I never claimed to be a saint." He waggled his eyebrows at her.

"You are so guilty."

"As charged." He winked at her. "And fortunate

to have the most beautiful woman in Dallas as my partner in crime."

She shook her head at him. "You take shameless to a whole new level, as well."

"And to think it's one of my finer qualities." He grinned. "Trust me. It's downhill from there."

She burst out laughing, and he was struck all over again by her loveliness — and not just on the inside. Only a few minutes into their visit, and she'd already proven to be witty, intelligent, empathetic, kindhearted, and blatantly honest. *Shoot!* She was, by far, the best investment he'd ever made.

The thought was immediately followed by a recoil of guilt, along with the realization that he didn't want her at his side throughout the weekend simply because he was paying her to be there. He liked her, plain and simple, and he was enjoying her company. Not to mention, he was majorly attracted to her. It was shaping up to be a great weekend, despite his concerns about the Pack and their occasional unwelcome opinions.

"So how is this going to work?" His fake bride started fidgeting with her handbag again.

"Oh, right." He dug in the pocket of his trousers and came up with a black felt box. "Wedding ring time." He popped open the lid. "It belonged to my mother. So, ah, guard it with your life."

A pained expression wafted across her features. "Oh, Mr. Keller! I couldn't possibly—"

"You should probably practice using my first name," he interrupted. "We'll be Ransom and Serena Keller the moment we step out of the car at my reunion."

"But you're asking me to wear a family heirloom!" she protested.

"I don't see the problem." Even though it wasn't a real marriage, he felt a little foolish holding a ring that the woman he'd hired to wear was refusing to put on. Looked like his poor record with women was holding with a vengeance.

"Listen," her voice sounded strained, "I'm not trying to be difficult. It's just that I recently lost my adoptive mother to cancer, and I never knew my real one, so I'd hate to be responsible for something so valuable. Something so irreplaceable."

He raised his brows. "It's insured."

"I wasn't referring to the price tag."

"I know." The best part about it is that it would give her instant credibility with the Pack. They'd known his mother, so they would recognize the ring.

She sighed. "You really don't have another ring for me to wear?"

"I really don't, so if you'll please keep your end of the bargain and put it on."

"Bargain?" She bit her lower lip and held out her hand.

"It was in the contract Iris drew up for me."

"Oh." Her fingers were shaking slightly as he slid

the ring on. It was an unexpectedly perfect fit. They both stared at it, speechless for a moment.

"Wow!" She gave a breathless little chuckle. "You'd think it was a real proposal, considering the attack of nerves I'm having over here."

He was taken aback to note a thin sheen of tears clouding her gaze. Attack of nerves, his hide! Putting on his mother's ring was upsetting her for reasons entirely unrelated to him. He was sure of it.

"I'm sorry if someone you cared for hurt you, Serena."

"Am I that transparent?" she moaned, fluttering her hand so that all two carats of the princess-cut diamond caught the shimmering rays of sunset.

"To someone who's also been hurt, yes."

She blinked damp lashes. "Well, if you can handle a little more transparency, it's someone I dated for an entire year. Then I found out he was cheating on me. We broke up a month ago."

"I'm sorry." Hearing the cause of her sadness made his blood boil. No woman deserved to be treated like that, especially someone as nice as Serena Chandler. Her ex had to be a complete loser. "Not that you asked for my opinion, but you probably dodged a bullet there." *Cheaters gonna cheat.*

"Iris said the same thing, but..." She expelled a breath, waving both hands at her face to dry her tears.

"It still hurts," he agreed. "I get it. Believe me. I

dated the same girl all four years of high school. Then she turned me down flat when I proposed." He shook his head. "There's been no one else since. Well, other than an occasional blind date now and then. Nothing serious."

Serena dabbed at the edges of her eyes. "I hear you. Blind dates are the worst!"

They shared a companionable chuckle over that. Then her voice grew quiet. "If this was a contest about who got hurt the most, though, you'd have me beat. At least, my ex and I only dated a year."

"It's not a contest," he assured quickly. There was no doubt in his mind that she'd been hurt just as deeply. Otherwise, she wouldn't have tears in her eyes.

"This whole weekend is about her, isn't it?" she pressed in that same quiet tone.

"Not really." He shrugged. "It's been twenty years. Pretty sure I'm long since over her." At the moment, he was so distracted by his damp-eyed, fake wife, he was actually having trouble conjuring up Macy Parker's image.

"If you say so." Her voice turned teasing. "I've got this niggling suspicion, though, that I'm about to get thrown into the role of a jealous wife."

"Now that you mention it, that's not a shabby idea." His gaze narrowed in speculation on her. "Originally, I was thinking of playing us off as a comfortable old married couple, but pretending to be newlyweds might be more fun for both of us. What do you prefer?"

"Newlyweds, for sure." They reached the next stoplight. The moment the vehicle came to a complete halt, she unlatched her seatbelt and moved across the aisle to join him in his seat. Buckling herself in beside him, she fixed him with a pouty look. "Promise me I have nothing to worry about with your ex, Ransom!" For emphasis, she rested her hand lightly on his arm after she finished.

He glanced down at her hand, liking the way his mother's diamond sparkled on her finger. "Hey, you're really good at this. Let me guess. You're a theater major like your friend." It wouldn't have been his first guess, but she was apparently full of surprises.

"Hardly." Her rosy lips quirked upward. "I'm studying Biostatistics."

"Sounds painful," he teased.

"Only for the competition." She lowered her voice conspiratorially. "I'm very good at online marketing research. I'm going to take StarCorp to new heights when I trade in my internship for a full-time position on their team."

He nodded in approval at the new picture forming in his mind. "So I get to be the hooah soldier who's crazy proud of his brainiac bride. I like it." He also liked how close they were sitting and the way her heart-shaped face remained tipped up to his. All he would have to do is lean down a few inches to brush his mouth against hers.

A crazy thought popped to the surface — that he might not still be a single guy if his path had crossed Serena Chandler's a few days sooner. He studied her intently. "Now that our length of marriage is decided, we have roughly five minutes left to get to know everything else there is to know about each other."

"Everything, huh? In only five minutes?"

"The important stuff, at least," he teased.

"Fair enough. I'm terrified of heights," she confessed, wrinkling her perfect nose at him.

He reached over to tap the tip of it. "Well, I jump out of airplanes for the fun of it. Guess it's one of those opposites-attract things."

She pursed her lips. "I'm more comfortable in a business suit than a cocktail dress, and I aspire to become the CEO of my own company someday."

"Speaking of dresses, my new favorite color is that shade of blue you're wearing."

Her cheeks pinked as she self-consciously smoothed a hand across her knee. "I borrowed it from Iris, along with everything else in my suitcase. She was pretty insistent on the fact that your high school reunion called for something besides running shorts and sneakers."

He raised his eyebrows at her. "Hope you ignored her advice and brought at least one pair of each. According to my itinerary, there's a charity run at the park in the morning."

"Do you run?" She frowned as she glanced down at his knee, making him wonder if she'd noticed his limp. For the life of him he couldn't figure out how, since all he'd done was open the car door and climb in after her.

"I can squeak out a few miles, no problem." He hated how defensive he sounded.

"I know it's not any of my business, but I can tell your knee is hurting from the way you keep rubbing it." She looked concern. "We don't have to do the run, if you've got a pulled muscle or something."

He was grudgingly impressed by how perceptive she was. Yeah, his leg had been hurting him all day. He planned to take a pain killer before the dance began, because he sure as heck wasn't missing the opportunity to twirl his fake bride around the ball-room. "It's an old injury, one I picked up in Afghanistan."

She looked more intrigued than sympathetic, a response he found refreshing. "In that case, I'll try to go easy on you out there on the dance floor, but no promises."

For the second time during the car ride, his gaze dropped to her sassy lips. "Limp or no limp, I can dance, lady. You're going to spend the evening trying to keep up. Trust me."

"Game on," she shot back with a wicked smile.

CHAPTER 3: OLD FLAMES BURN BRIGHT

SERENA

Serena was enjoying her status as a fake bride way more than she'd anticipated. If she had to come up with one word to describe Sergeant Ransom Keller, it would be *awesome*. If she could make it two words, it would be *seriously awesome*. During their twenty-minute drive across Dallas, he'd lived up to every single line item on his resume and profile.

Hunky, ripped soldier.

Check.

Decorated war veteran.

Check.

Extreme sports enthusiast and thrill seeker.

Check.

And like the icing on the proverbial cake, he was also a selfless public servant.

Checkity check!

And don't even get her started on his gorgeous eyes! After he pulled off his aviator sunglasses, she'd discovered they were a delicious shade of dark chocolate, nearly the same shade as his hair. Add in the fact that he was as hilarious as all get-out, super fun to be around, and hotter than the fires he put out for a living, she was genuinely looking forward to spending the weekend with him.

Serena waffled between hoping Ransom's ex would and would not show up at the reunion. On one hand, she had no desire to witness any scabs being pulled off and old wounds reopened. On the other hand, she sort of relished the idea of playing the part of a jealous wife. If it came to that, she fully intended to rub his ex's nose in the fact that he'd moved on.

They had to wind their way through a maze of upscale hotel hallways and lounges to reach the Rio Grande Palace ballroom. A pair of tables draped in white linen stretched across the entrance to the double doors leading into the ballroom. A cheerful banner draped across the tables proclaimed they'd reached the reunion check-in area.

A platinum blonde in a white dress with a scoop neck was leaning over the roster. If Serena had to guess, the woman's slightly orange tan was straight from a bottle. Either that, or it was one of those spray on deals, because the skin on the back of her hands looked a little splotchy. There was also an indention around her ring finger, as if she'd recently removed a wedding band. Her name was scrolled in wide, loopy letters on her stick-on badge. *Macy Parker.*

The way Ransom's shoulders stiffened and his features went blank told Serena all she needed to know about the woman's identity.

You've got to be kidding me! There was nothing like bumping into his ex before they so much as stepped on the dance floor. Talk about rotten luck!

"Ransom Keller," Macy cooed, leaning forward a little. Her lips seemed to be permanently half-puckered, making Serena wonder if she'd paid for a Botox treatment.

By now, the woman was displaying such a disturbing amount of cleavage that Serena glanced away momentarily. *Sheesh, lady! Leave something to the imagination, will you?*

"A bunch of folks have been placing bets about who your latest plus one is." Her gaze raked critically over Serena's dress. "So what's the flavor of the day? Your administrative assistant?" Her puffy lips turned downward. "No, wait. I think I've got it. You're dating your personal trainer," she crowed in triumph as she eyed Serena's slender waistline.

Latest plus one? Flavor of the day? From Serena's standpoint, it sounded like a laughably un-subtle attempt to spoil her ex's evening. *Get a life, will ya?* Maybe it was petty to feel this way, but she also resented the dig about her size. The only reason she was so thin was because she was poor. Period.

She thought it was strange how Macy was attacking them so openly, too. It was no wonder Ransom had gone to the trouble to rent a date for the weekend. His large hand settled against the small of her back, both soothing and steadying her. It also reminded her of their mission.

"I guess you haven't heard." She abruptly thrust her hand beneath Macy's overly inquisitive nose, fluttering her ring finger for good measure. "I'm the permanent kind of plus one."

"You got married? Since when?" The pen Macy was holding slid from her fingers, and her puffy lips rounded in an O of shock. She straightened in her chair and looked at Ransom for confirmation.

The woman's dramatic reaction left Serena wondering if she still harbored feelings for the man she'd sent packing years ago. Who knew? Maybe she'd finally realized her mistake and was hoping to make things right between them after all this time. Working the sign-in desk sure was a clever way to ensure their paths crossed again.

"Even hard hearts have their breaking points," Ransom drawled. He reached for Serena's hand and laced his fingers through hers. Lifting their joined hands, he brushed his mouth against her knuckles. "I guess you could say Serena Keller was mine."

Though Serena knew they were merely playing a

role, her heart raced at the warmth of his mouth against her skin. She stifled a shiver of acute awareness. "As the old saying goes, the bigger they are, the harder they fall."

Ransom's gaze locked on hers with such intensity that they might as well have been the only two people standing there.

Her breathing grew shallow. The contract he'd signed with Iris's Rent-A-Date service had specifically stated no public displays of affection would be required other than simple hand holding. However, the rules of the game suddenly seemed in flux.

Not that Serena minded. There was just something about Ransom Keller that made her want to help fight his battles. Everything from his uniform, to his limp, to his old-fashioned charm.

Macy expelled a breath. "As Ransom's classmate, I've definitely had the pleasure of seeing him fall a time or two." She glanced slyly at Serena. "Or three." She angrily scrawled their names on a pair of stick-on badges and shoved them across the table.

There was no mistaking the venom in her tone. She was clearly trying to make Ransom sound like a player.

Serena couldn't resist one final jab of her own. "So long as I'm the last time he falls," she murmured.

Their gazes clashed and held as awareness zinged between them.

Out of the corner of her eye, she saw Macy

jerkily bend to retrieve a pair of fluorescent yellow t-shirts from the row of boxes beneath the check-in table. "These are for tomorrow's run. Wearing them is optional, but you get to keep them as a souvenir. You'll get your number assigned when you check in." The words came out in a rush, as if she was anxious to get through the line and send them on their way.

Serena swallowed a chuckle as she noticed the size on her shirt label — large. "You don't, by any chance, have any small sizes left?"

"We didn't order any smalls," Macy bit out. "I might have a medium, though," she conceded in a milder voice.

"That would be fantastic!"

Macy stiffly swapped out the shirt. Then her gaze latched on to the next person in line. "Oh, hi, Matt! Long time, no see." It was as if she'd forgotten all about Ransom and Serena's presence, though the twin red spots riding her cheeks said otherwise.

Ransom spun around. "Well, if it isn't the one and only Matt Cherokee!"

"He-e-e-y, you!" A hulk of a guy engulfed Ransom in a bear hug. The slaps the two men gave each other's backs were as loud as thunder.

Over Ransom's shoulder, Matt's dark gaze landed on Serena. "Whoa! So this is the mysterious plus one." He gave a long, low whistle. "I can see why you've been keeping her all to yourself."

Ransom stepped back to rejoin Serena, slinging

an arm around her middle. "This is my wife, Serena."

"Your what?" His friend pretended to wring water out of his ears. "I could've sworn you said wife, but I don't recall receiving an invitation to your wedding." His dark gaze swept over her with a mixture of admiration and envy.

"Small, private ceremony, bro. Like you said, I wanted her all to myself."

"What did you do? Elope to Vegas?"

To Serena's relief, Ransom ignored Matt's attempt to dig for details. There hadn't been time on the ride over to fabricate much in the way of a back story.

"Matt Cherokee was our top lineman." Ransom bent his head closer to Serena's ear to whisper loudly. "If he sounds a little whacked, it's because he probably got tackled one too many times on our way to the state championship play-offs four years straight."

Matt cheered noisily and dragged Ransom into a crazy, long, and complicated handshake.

"Got a family?" Ransom asked after he and Matt tapped their fists together one last time.

"Not even a girlfriend." His friend tilted his head cockily. "You know me. Never had any trouble landing a date. Just don't have any luck keeping 'em once they get to know me."

His words made Ransom's expression grow

somber. "There's someone for everyone out there, bro." He clapped him on the shoulder again.

"So it would seem." Matt shook his head, a disbelieving expression staining his tanned features. "Guess you're proof enough of that. Married, after all this time! Can't believe we're going to have to kick you out of the singles club."

"Good!" Macy, who they'd pretty much been ignoring, took the opportunity to jump back into the conversation. "I'm happy to take his place." She fluttered her red-lacquered fingernails to draw attention to her bare ring finger. "Recently divorced and happy to be free of the ol' ball and chain again." She shot Ransom a mocking look.

"Sorry to hear it." He looked disinterested. "If you'll excuse us, I promised my bride a whirl around the dance floor." He reached for Serena's hand again.

"Not quite, sweetie." She laughed up at him, warming to her role. "You mainly bragged about showing me your moves. I believe your exact words were, *try to keep up.*"

"So, how long did you say you two have been married?" Macy's laugh took on a shrill edge.

"I didn't say. I just assumed it was obvious." Ransom shrugged as he nudged Serena toward the ballroom doors. "We're newlyweds."

"Well, enjoy the dance," she trilled after them, "and his moves, such as they are."

"Unbelievable," Ransom muttered as they stepped inside the ballroom together.

"Hell hath no fury like a woman scorned," Serena returned softly, glancing around.

"Hey, she's the one who walked away from me."

"Her loss," she scoffed and was surprised when Ransom's fingers tightened on hers.

"Thanks for saying that, even if you don't mean it."

"I do mean it. She's a real piece of work. Like a really nice guy said to me earlier this evening, I think you dodged a bullet there."

"Yep. I was the proverbial young and dumb where she was concerned." He shook his head. "But no longer."

She assumed that was his way of saying he was over Macy, but she wasn't convinced. "They say you never entirely forget your first love," she reminded in a bemused voice.

"Maybe not." He grimaced. "Still doesn't change the fact that I've outgrown her."

That works for me. Serena's heart did a little two-step at his candor. "That's a good way of putting it." Not too long ago, she'd considered herself head-over-heels in love, too.

He studied her with a curious brand of intensity. "Makes the whole prospect of marriage twice as terrifying when you take into consideration just how much people can change over time."

She gave him a wry smile. "And yet, foolish girls like me persist in believing in love."

"I don't think it's foolish." They moved across the crowded dance floor together.

"Thanks. Just for the record, I agree that people change, but maybe there's still hope for love. Maybe you just have to find someone who's moving in the same direction, you know?"

His smile was starting to do crazy things to her heart. "I'll settle for dancing in the same direction, if you're game."

"I am."

She allowed him to take her in his arms and give her an experimental twirl. She took the opportunity to tip her head back and gaze around the brightly lit room. It was bathed in the glow of thousands of tiny white lights suspended from the ceiling. Round dining tables lined the outer perimeter of the ballroom, draped in classic white linen. Wide crystal votives of varying heights served as centerpieces, from which burning red lilypad candles floated.

"It's so beautiful!" Serena gushed, reveling in the faint chirp of birds and hum of crickets that ensued while the band transitioned from one number to the next. "Truly magical." The planners of his school's twentieth reunion had designed the event down to a meticulous level of detail that was truly impressive.

"I agree." Ransom gave her another twirl. The

music burst into a Latino rhythm, and he skillfully sashayed with her through a set of basic salsa steps.

She rested one hand on his shoulder, still holding her tiny beaded handbag. The other hand she placed in his upraised hand, and quickly discovered he hadn't been joking about his moves. Not even a little. Ransom Keller could dance so well that his limp was virtually unnoticeable.

"You're an incredible dancer!" she exclaimed breathlessly when the music transitioned again.

"I have my moments." He reached up to tuck back a strand of her hair that had come loose.

His fingers brushed the shell of her ear, eliciting a new wave of awareness between them. "You're no stranger to the dance floor, either, Mrs. Keller." He leaned closer to say her fake married name directly in her ear, pulling a merry chuckle from her.

"Oh, hey!" He straightened suddenly. "There's Remy and Tucker. Two more Pack members I'd like you to meet."

This time, she resisted the tug of his hand.

He raised his brows "Is everything okay?"

"Yes. It's just that we haven't had time to polish up our back stories. Do you really think it's wise to charge over there and expose ourselves to more questions?"

"Yes." His brown eyes twinkled down at her. "You're so much fun to be with, that I'm kind of just enjoying making it up as we go."

You think I'm fun? Serena had been called a lot of things in the past, to include nerdy and overly serious. But fun? That was a new one for her. "Okay, then." She drew a deep breath and offered him a tremulous smile. "This is me, wishing I'd paid more attention during the improv part of my undergrad Speech class."

He bent his knees a few times and rolled his neck. "Just follow my lead, darlin'. I'm kind of an expert at making garbage up, which any of my classmates will happily affirm."

They were still chuckling when they reached his friends.

Remy Carrington eyed her with open curiosity as they were introduced. However, he didn't hesitate to hold out his hand. "Wow! You married up, Keller." His tone was so matter-of-fact that Serena laughed again.

"Look who's talking." Ransom's hand settled possessively on her waist.

"Can't deny that." The sandy-haired linebacker wasn't as tall as Ransom and Matt, but he was built like a solid wall. He also had a very pregnant wife tucked against his side. "This is Jenn. We're expecting our first baby." He beamed with pride at her.

"We?" The lovely Asian woman made a face at him and playfully swatted his chest. "Kind of feels like I'm doing most of the heavy lifting here."

He snorted. "Probably because you're carrying the next Camden Hall champion linebacker."

His words were met by the jeers of his friends.

His wife waited until they subsided. Then she shook back her long, dark hair. "If that's the case, you may need to pitch in a little more."

"Another foot rub, darling?" He kissed the top of her head.

"Ha! You can play with my toes in the hospital, mister." She batted her lashes at him. "Right now, I could use a little help dancing this baby out."

Remy gave an exaggerated sigh of long-suffering. "Duty calls," he grumbled to no one in particular, not looking the least put out as he twirled his beautiful wife onto the dance floor.

"Good riddance! Maybe I can finally get a word in." Ransom's other friend, who had waited in silence while Remy introduced his wife, called after the departing Remy. He ran a hand through his spiked blonde hair, pushing the strands to even more chaotic angles. "After twenty years, that guy is still a motor mouth."

"Hey, it works for me." Remy, who wasn't yet out of earshot, dipped his wife in their direction and rubbed her belly suggestively.

Serena clapped a hand over her mouth, trying not to laugh while Jenn gave a squeal of outrage.

"You did *not* just rub my belly to make a point with your old football bud—"

He cut off her tirade by sealing his mouth over hers.

"Show off," the spiked blonde-haired fellow grumbled, turning away from the happy couple. "I'm Tucker Holmes, by the way," he announced to Serena. "Guess I'm not going to get a red carpet introduction like the others." His scowl in Ransom's direction held none of Remy's earlier teasing.

"The others? What others?" Ransom looked surprised by the jab.

"Macy said you and Matt enjoyed quite the reunion at the welcome desk."

"The Bible according to Macy Parker, eh?"

Tucker had the grace to look a tad uncomfortable.

"Don't suppose you have any idea why a non-Camden Hall grad is working our check-in table this time around." He scowled back. "Instead of a member of our student council, President Holmes."

He shrugged. "You know how lazy I am. She offered, and I jumped at the chance to get out of work. No mystery there."

"So my theory that the two of you are together now is way off?"

"Good question." Tucker made twin pistols out of his thumbs and forefingers and aimed them in Ransom and Serena's direction. "If you really want to know the answer to that, you'll need to join the

Pack for a round of Truth Or Dare." He winked, relaxing a few degrees. "For old time's sake."

"Oh, come on!" Ransom protested. "We're not fifteen any more."

Tucker ignored him. "The dean allowed us to reserve the school gym. The old, original one with the wood floor."

"For a generous bribe, I bet?"

His friend shrugged. "It's called a donation, slick. To the alumni fund."

Ransom grimaced. "Tomato. To-mah-to."

"Exactly." Tucker jabbed a finger in the air. "Eleven o'clock tomorrow morning. You'll need to skip the charity race brunch. We'll be catering in real food for a real after party."

"At least it's not Spin the Bottle," Ransom grumbled. "Remy and I are married men now."

"We considered it." Tucker's expression turned cagey.

"So a game of Truth or Dare, eh?" Ransom sighed. "I can't believe I'm letting you talk me into this."

"Not just you." Tucker waggled a finger between him and Serena. "Both of you. Plus Ones are not only welcome, but highly encouraged to attend."

Great. Just great. Serena wondered if she was imagining the icy edge to Tucker's gaze when he issued the invitation. Had Macy passed on her suspicions about Ransom's shotgun wedding to him? If so, it looked like Ransom's game of improv was just about over.

The fake Mr. and Mrs. Keller were going to have to put their heads back together and quick to fabricate a believable back story about how they'd met and fallen for each other.

CHAPTER 4: FAKE IT OR MAKE IT

RANSOM

"Has anyone seen Owen?" According to their online class message board, all five members of the Pack were expected to be in attendance at the homecoming dance. However, Matt, Remy, and Tucker were the only ones Ransom had laid eyes on so far.

Tucker lifted a hand to his chest, pretending distress. "Ouch! If you haven't seen Owen, that means he hasn't yet pressed you into service for his upcoming flash mob routine."

"Sorry I asked." Ransom snorted, afraid to hear what was coming next.

"So what he needs us to do is rush the stage when the new dean starts his speech."

Ransom chuckled. "I've never met the fellow. Whatever did he to do to get on Owen's bad side?"

"He insisted on blocking off twenty blasted minutes for his welcome speech at nine o'clock tonight. You know Owen isn't going to stand for someone wind-bagging that long at our reunion, especially some stuffed shirt who never had anything to do with our class."

Ransom couldn't have agreed more. "I'm in." He fist-bumped Tucker, and they exchanged conspiratorial glances just like old times. "Huddle up, team." Falling back into his role as a football captain, he crooked an arm at Serena to include her. "Come on, darlin'. As my favorite partner in crime, I hereby christen you an honorary member of the Pack for the duration of one flash mob performance." He winked at her. "Afterward, you'll revert to the role of my beloved wife."

"Well, that's some fine writing for you." She stuck her tongue out at him. "It's definitely the first time I've ever been offered a promotion with the promise of an immediate demotion. What's in it for me, sergeant? Besides the demotion, of course." She tapped the toe of her crystal studded sandal as she awaited his reply.

Ransom was entranced by her constant ability to dish it back to him. For a woman who'd never before participated in a Rent-A-Date contract, she was turning out to be a natural at this role playing stuff. He sincerely hoped it had something to do with the attraction he felt blossoming between them.

Then again, he'd never rented a date before, either. Maybe he was being foolish to allow his feelings to become involved in any way with a woman who might be doing nothing more than what he was paying her to do — act.

He suddenly longed to test those acting abilities. To see if he could shock her into a genuine response of some sort — one so genuine that even he couldn't question it.

"How does a trip to Venice sound, babe?" He dipped his head to look deeply into her eyes. "I never got to take you on a real honeymoon, and well, I kind of like the idea of paddling my bride around the city of love in a Gondola."

Her toe immediately stopped tapping. She blinked at him a few times. Then her eyes misted. "Italy?" she breathed. "Oh, Ransom!" Her voice broke.

Without thinking, he held his arms out to her. He didn't know what he'd done wrong, only that he intended to fix it — no matter what, even if he blew their cover to Kingdom Come. In that moment, it no longer mattered what the Pack thought about his hasty wedding. He just needed things to be alright between him and the most amazing woman he'd ever met.

To his relief, Serena stepped wordlessly into his arms.

He gathered her close and rubbed a hand in gentle circles across her back. "Talk to me," he whispered against her cheek. "Tell me what I did wrong."

"I've always wanted to go to Italy." Her voice shook. "We couldn't afford it, not in a million years. That said, my mother and I used to joke about going...before the cancer took her." Her voice faded beneath the music filling the room.

Over her head, Ransom caught Tucker's curious gaze and shook his head at him. *Not now,* he mouthed to his friend.

Looking disgusted, Tucker threw his hands in the air and backed away. "Nine o'clock," he snarled.

Ransom gave him a thumbs up, hoping a half hour would be enough time to set things straight with Serena. Uncaring who else might be watching them, he wrapped his arms more tightly around her. *Man!* Losing a parent to cancer was awful. "When you get back to school on Monday, I want you to take a hard look at your calendar, darlin'." He spoke low in her ear. "We'll make that trip in her honor, okay?"

"Please stop," she rasped, twisting in his arms to dart a furtive look around them. No longer seeing Tucker, she tipped her face up to his. "I'm trying really hard to stay in character here, but you hit a real nerve."

"I know, and I'm sorry."

"It's not your fault. There's no way you could've known." To his agony, a tear streaked down her face. Then another. "If we were really a couple, there's no place you could have offered to take me that would have meant more."

He reached up to brush the dampness from her cheek with his thumbs. "If you agree to date me after this weekend is over, we could make this thing we seem to have going on a real thing."

"Wow! A pity proposal, huh?" Her expression turned indignant, her eyes snapping blue fire.

Her response both impressed and amused him, though he didn't feel the least bit like laughing. "Really, Serena? I'm thirty-seven years old. I think I know what I'm looking for in a relationship by now." Her, as a matter of fact. He was looking for someone exactly like her. Someone sweet and sassy. Someone ridiculously intelligent. Someone he was suddenly sure he would never get tired of talking to or being with.

She shook her head in exasperation at him. "I think you're forgetting how much money you just finished dropping on one of Iris's Rent-A-Date contracts. It didn't sound to me like you were looking for much of a commitment."

"I wasn't," he admitted, opting for flat-out honesty. She deserved no less. "Then you stepped into my life in that stunning blue dress of yours and rocked my world."

"It's a borrowed dress," she clarified in a milder tone. Her expression remained grave. "The label on it is way above my pay grade. To be perfectly honest, this hotel we're standing in, your prep school friends, and the entire weekend you have planned is above my pay grade." More tears gathered in her eyes. "I should have never agreed to something so outrageous. I don't know what I was think—"

At a loss for how to convince a woman that he'd just met that his feelings for her were becoming all too real, he did the first thing that came to mind. He bent his head over hers and stopped her self-deprecatory tirade with a kiss.

She gave a little gasp. Then her lips moved beneath his.

His heart pounded at the realization she was kissing him back, and there was no faking that. Kissing wasn't part of their contract. Kissing was extra. It was off script. It was real.

It was also a little mind-blowing to find himself necking like a teenager in the middle of his twentieth high school reunion. Grateful that the lighting was dim, he reluctantly ended the best kiss of his life. However, he was unable to let her go just yet. He touched his forehead to hers, craving her nearness. Her sweetness.

"Does this mean you're agreeing to be my girl?" He breathed in her intoxicating scent — a heady mixture of lip gloss and some sort of flowery perfume. "For real this time?" He couldn't have cared less about what their stupid dating contract said, at this point.

"Yes." She gave a breathy chuckle that tugged his

heart in at least six different directions. "If you're not afraid of being snagged on the rebound."

Afraid? He snorted. "There's not much I'm afraid of, darlin'."

"Well, you should be, Ransom. We barely know each other, so we have no idea what we're getting ourselves into. In case you haven't figured it out yet, I'm a wreck. Still grieving over the loss of my mom, still messed up in the head over my recent break-up, and a starving college student, to boot."

He stopped her renewed tirade by tracing a thumb over her lower lip. "Be my wreck, Serena Chandler."

A tiny sob escaped her. "What?"

"I just want to be with you. I'm not sure I can explain it to your brainiac satisfaction. You're just going to have to take my word for it."

"Ransom! You're asking me to take a pretty big leap of faith here."

"If you think another kiss would help clear up the matter, I'm game," he teased.

"Maybe," she shot back, sounding so frustrated that he grinned.

He hugged her, still grinning. "Believe me, I want to. Badly. But I'm trying to show you a little more respect than that. Something tells me that public maulings aren't normally your thing."

"They're not." A breathless giggle escaped her. "You're pretty awesome, you know?"

The music switched to something slow and mellow. He gently rocked her back and forth in time to the beat. "Yep, that's what all the ladies tell me."

"Except for Macy, huh?"

He gave a bark of laughter as he cuddled her closer.

She smiled damply up at him. "Seriously, though, I really, really like you. You know what that means, don't you?"

He had no idea. "Let me guess. It's going to snow tomorrow?" He dipped her low over his arm.

Her eyes widened with mirth. "In September?"

He pulled her upright. "You're talking to a guy who's busy falling for his fake bride. If that can happen, anything can happen."

Her expression turned all soft and vulnerable, making him ache to kiss her again.

"Well, here's one thing that's *not* going to happen," she declared matter-of-factly. "I won't be collecting any money from you for this weekend. It wouldn't be right if we're going to start dating."

Wow! Could she be any more wonderful? He knew she needed the money, though, so there was no way he was taking it back. "Too late. I already wired the funds to your friend." Technically, he'd only paid her half. The rest was due at the end of the weekend. "That means you're technically still on the clock, Mrs. Keller. Sorry, but you don't get to go back to being Serena Chandler until Monday." Maybe if he kept the fake bride gig going a little longer, she'd let the money issue go. Or so he hoped.

"You seriously want to keep playing the married game?" She wrinkled her nose at him, looking puzzled.

With you? Absolutely! "What can I say? I'm having a really great time tonight." He twirled her a few times, relieved that she wasn't putting up too much of a fight about the money. Then he tugged her close again.

"You're a nut."

"I'll be anything you want me to be, Serena."

Looking wistful, she twined her arms around his neck. "If this turns out to be something more than some ill-advised weekend fling that we both wake up cringing about on Monday..."

"Ouch!" He didn't bother hiding his wince.

"Relax! I was just going to say you may very well be the best thing that's ever happened to me, Ransom Keller."

"Right back atcha, Mrs. Keller." Unable to resist her soft lips and hopeful smile any longer, he swooped in for their second kiss.

It felt like coming home. Years of loneliness fled beneath her shy, questing mouth and gentle touch. She was such a beautiful person on every level. His heart swelled with amazement and gratitude to be the guy she'd agreed to date. She seriously checked all the boxes of everything he'd ever wanted in a woman. Everything he'd been missing in his life. It was way too bad it had taken them this long to meet and start dating. However, she was, quite simply, worth the wait.

The music crescendoed to a grand finale in the background, warning him that the nine o'clock hour was approaching. He lifted his head, feeling downright intoxicated with happiness.

"You need to start telling jokes or something." His voice came out gravelly with emotion.

"Or what?" she chuckled, eyes shining with wonder into his.

"Or I'm going to kiss you every time you look at me that way, darlin'."

She smoothed her hands across his shoulder cuffs. "Okay. How about this one? An anaconda, a hummingbird, and an octopus walked into a coffee shop..."

He raised his eyebrows at her, snorting with laughter. "Yeah, I really don't see that happening. For starters, none of them can walk."

"But you laughed, because it was stupidly funny."

"Okay, you got my attention. What's the rest of it?"

"That was it." She smiled triumphantly.

"But you didn't finish the joke."

"I didn't have to. You were already laughing. Mic

drop." She stepped back from his embrace and gave him a mocking curtsey.

He snickered. "You might want to stick to Biostatistics, darlin'."

"But I'm starting to like improv." She sashayed a few more steps even though the music had come to an end. "With a little practice, I might be able to turn it into a side hustle."

Don't get your hopes up. "Uh-huh."

The new dean of Camden Hall chose that moment to take the microphone. "Good evening, ladies and gentlemen, faculty, and honored guests. I'm Dr. Grant Penhurst, and I'm happy to welcome you to the opening night of your twentieth class reunion. I know I've never had the pleasure of meeting most of you personally, but—"

Owen Bayfield ran onto the stage, barking like a dog. He was wearing a blue police uniform, a silver badge as large as a dinner plate, and dark glasses. Despite his costume, there was no denying it was him because of his crazy red beard and unruly red waves.

The ballroom full of Camden Hall alumni, whose expressions had started to glaze over beneath Dr. Penhurst's nasally presentation, burst into cheers as they perceived they were being rescued by their beloved Pack.

Owen snatched up the dean's microphone and shouted into it, "Who let the dogs out?"

The music started up again.

"I said, who let the dogs out?"

Ransom glanced over at Serena. She was laughing and clapping like the rest of the crowd, thoroughly enjoying the replay of one of the biggest pop singles of his senior year of high school.

That's my girl. He danced her closer to the stage, joining in Owen's singing. "Who let the dogs out?"

She sang back. "Who, who, who, who, who?"

He leaned closer to her. "Who let the dogs out?"

This time, she started jiving to the music as she sang the words back, "Who, who, who, who, who?"

Watching her in delight, those standing around them joined in the song, rocking back and forth to the beat. Moments later, more dancers joined them. A few classmates pulled out their cell phones and pretended they were singing into walkie talkies. In less than a minute, the whole ballroom had erupted into a singing, dancing frenzy.

To his credit, the dean watched in bemusement for a minute or two. Then, to the delight of the crowd, he unbuttoned his somber black blazer, tossed it across the stage, and joined in the dancing.

"Best! Reunion! Ever!" someone shouted.

Ransom agreed, but it was more than that. The opening festivities also marked the day he'd met the girl of his dreams. It was way too soon to drop the L word on her, but tonight was the start of something very special. Something lasting. He was sure of it.

Wanting to end it on a high note, and — he might as well admit it — wanting Serena all to himself for a while, he purposefully maneuvered her toward the ballroom exit as they danced.

He caught her laughing gaze and angled his head toward the door. "Wanna get out of here?"

She nodded, and he reached for her hand. Fingers laced, they slipped from the room while the party was still in full swing. The sign-in booth was empty now. Only a few classmates loitered in the wide hallway, pacing back and forth while speaking on cell phones.

Pegging them for executives who were chained to their jobs, Ransom didn't envy them one bit. Short of a major fire breaking out in downtown Dallas, he was taking the entire weekend off.

And he planned to spend every waking second of it getting to know his amazing new girlfriend better.

CHAPTER 5: THE LIES THEY TELL

SERENA

Serena's shyness returned as she and Ransom stepped inside the glassed-in elevator leading to the top floor.

After spending the last few hours in a ballroom full of people, it was more than a little breathtaking to find herself alone with him again.

The guy she'd pretended to be married to for the past several hours. The guy she'd agreed to start dating on Monday.

The powerful sense of awareness that had been between them all evening escalated. So did the anticipation.

She leaned back against one of the mirrored walls, more than ready to kick off her high-heeled sandals. They were well made and boasted memory foam soles. However, four-inch heels were, quite simply, not meant to be worn for any longer than absolutely necessary.

Ransom was leaning against the opposite wall of the elevator, studying her with a slightly dazed expression.

She gave an inward shiver at how darkly handsome he was. All tanned and ripped and capable looking. He filled out his dress blues very nicely. She also liked the purple heart award hanging against his chest and the crescent badge emblazoned on his shoulder that read *SPECIAL FORCES*. It was both exhilarating and humbling to realize she was in the presence of a real war hero.

One she'd had the honor of kissing more than once.

He waggled his brows teasingly at her. "Like what you see, Mrs. Keller?"

"Fishing for compliments, Sergeant Keller?"

"Yep."

She smiled. "I enjoyed the dance. You were right. You've got a few nice moves."

"I gave you fair warning, darlin'." He winked at her.

"Oh, is that what you call it?" she teased. "Guess I mistook it for shameless bragging."

He shrugged. "When you're good, you're good, lady."

She liked the fact that he enjoyed dancing. It was like defying everything he'd suffered — every moment of danger and every injury, including the one that had left him with a permanent limp. It was a celebration of life, itself.

The number of each floor they passed flashed across the light-up sign above the door. It came to a halt at the number twenty.

"Honey, we're home," Ransom sang out teasingly, pushing away from the mirrored wall. He withdrew a key from his pocket, opened a small silver door on the wall, which she hadn't noticed until now, and inserted the key. Only then did the doors roll open.

He waved his arm in a princely flourish to usher her out of the elevator ahead of him.

She winced as she stood upright on her heels again. "So this is the honeymoon suite, huh?"

"Yep! You're in for a real treat, darlin'."

She was amazed to discover they'd stepped directly into the penthouse, itself, from the elevator. He hadn't been kidding about the treat, either. With a sigh of sheer delight, she kicked off her heels.

They were standing in an elegant lounge area, with a pair of leather sofas and a scattering of over-stuffed chairs on an enormous Persian rug. One side of the room was a wall of glass overlooking the twinkling Dallas skyline. On the opposite wall was a stacked stone fireplace. A faux fire blazed from the other side of the glassed-in hearth.

"Bet those shoes were killing you." Ransom unbuttoned his blazer.

"Only for the past half hour or so," she quipped. "I'm pretty sure they come with an expiration date."

"You're my hero." Though his voice was joking, his expression was sympathetic.

"Says the man wearing a purple heart."

He inclined his head humbly. "So, ah...uniforms like these aren't much more comfortable to wear than stilettos. If you don't mind, I'd like to shower and change. Then we can meet back here to go over our game plan for tomorrow."

She gave him a two-fingered salute. "Whatever you say, Sergeant."

His eyebrows rose playfully. "Be careful what you offer, Mrs. Keller. If you give me a blank check, we might end up in another necking session."

She smiled shyly, hardly knowing what to say to that.

He angled his thumb across the lounge. "Your room is that way. The one overlooking the pool."

"Wow! I bet it looks like a tiny puddle from this far up."

"Not quite. I was referring to the rooftop pool."

"We have our own pool up here?" Her lips parted in surprise. It was difficult to wrap her mind around such luxury.

"That we do, Mrs. Keller, so if you happened to bring a swimsuit..."

"I have no idea what Iris packed for me," she confessed with a breathy laugh. "Nor any idea where my suitcase is, now that you mention it."

"I had it delivered to your room."

Of course, you did. She nodded in bemusement at the reminder she was dating a very wealthy man. One who'd attended a private, all-male, college preparatory academy. One who rented limousines and penthouse suites. One willing to invest a few thousand dollars in acquiring a fake bride for a single weekend — via a contract that specified no romantic involvement was required.

They'd ventured so far beyond the parameters of their original agreement that it was positively mind-boggling! Serena suddenly wondered what sort of expectations Ransom had of her now that they were dating.

And alone.

He drew a heavy breath. "Did I say something wrong?" He grimaced. "Again?"

"No, I..." She had no idea how to put her fears into words without sounding offensive.

"You know you can tell me anything, Mrs. Keller," he reminded in a light voice as he shrugged out of his jacket and dangled it from a finger over his shoulder. "We're married, remember? At least until the end of the weekend."

"About that," she sighed. "Things are changing so quickly between us that it's probably best if we revise the ground rules...especially now that we're alone." She blushed, knowing she probably sounded every shade of unsophisticated and unsure of herself.

His expression instantly sobered. "Remember what I said earlier about respecting you too much to maul you in public?"

She nodded.

"You have my word that I'll always respect you in private, as well." He held her gaze steadily. "Call me old-fashioned, but there are lines I don't believe in crossing outside of marriage. Who knows? Maybe my straight-lacedness is why I'm still single. However, I've reached the point where I'd rather be alone than to be with someone who doesn't respect my principles in return."

Wow! She regarded him in awe as she slid her thumb along the underside of her borrowed wedding band. "Thank you, Ransom. That's a set of ground rules I can wholeheartedly agree to." Even when her adoptive mother's health had spiraled downward, she'd never been one to stay home from church. Her faith had been very important to her, and it was equally important now to Serena.

"Good," Ransom's eyes crinkled at the corners as he smiled, "because I really like you, and I'd really like to see where things go between us."

"Me, too." Now that they'd cleared the air on one very important topic, she was much more at ease around him. "I just thought it would be best to be honest up front about things. I wasn't as transparent with my ex, and I think that's what led to our breakup."

"That, and the fact that he didn't deserve you," Ransom declared flatly. "It's one thing not to share the same principles with the person you're dating. It's another thing entirely to be a liar and a cheat."

She nodded, grimacing. "Thank you for saying for that. It helps." She'd spent way too much time lately, trying to figure out what she coulda woulda shoulda done differently to make things work between her and Victor. Ransom was right, though. Her ex was a dishonest person. As much as his betrayal had hurt, it was better for him to have shown his true colors before their relationship had gone any further.

"You're welcome." He regarded her warmly. "The right person is always worth waiting for, Serena. Never have I believed that more than I do right now."

She blushed. "In case you're wondering, I really like your old-fashioned manners. If my mother was still alive, I think she would've approved of me dating a guy like you."

"I hope so."

"I'll, ah..." she gestured in the direction of her bedroom, "guess I'd better go get changed, so we can get to work on that game plan we never got around to finishing earlier."

He glanced at his watch. "Want to meet me back here in, say, thirty minutes? Is that long enough for you?"

"It's perfect!" Stooping to retrieve her discarded sandals, she could feel his admiring gaze on her as she walked barefoot across the gleaming hardwood floor.

Every detail of the penthouse proved to be gasp-worthy. The hallway leading to her room contained a fountain gushing with water into a koi pond. Several large squares of the hallway floor were composed of thick, clear glass, which made it possible to watch the fish swimming beneath her feet from one side of the hallway to the other.

She slowed her steps, enjoying the peaceful sound of water falling and the flashes of orange and yellow colors as fish darted in and out of their greenery hideaways.

Her bedroom drew a squeal of bliss from her. For one thing, it was bigger than the entire apartment she shared with Iris. A round, king-sized bed with a rich blue and gold bedspread anchored the center of the room, which boasted two entire walls of glass. A sauna bubbled within a bayed-out area on one of the glass walls. Double doors led to a rooftop balcony on the other glass wall.

A bench at the foot of the bed boasted a wide crystal vase. Dozens of pink and red roses were arrayed in it, with green vines spilling over its rim. An ivory note rested beside the vase.

Infused with curiosity, Serena moved across the room to snatch it up and read it.

Thank you for being my wife. — RK

She pressed the note to her heart, amazed at what an utterly romantic weekend Ransom had planned for his fake bride. He'd put a lot of thought into the details. She slowly made her way to the credenza beside the bed, which her suitcase was resting beside.

Or rather her empty suitcase, as it turned out. Experimentally opening a few drawers of the credenza, she discovered someone had unpacked for her, neatly tucking away her clothing. *Talk about service!* If she'd ever wondered what it was like to be treated like a princess — and she had — now she knew.

She riffled through the items of clothing Iris had packed for her, and her heart sank. They were desperately short of anything she would normally wear. The only exceptions were the filmy black running shorts and hot pink tank top that she was probably supposed to wear to the charity run in the morning.

She examined and discarded the lacy white nightgown and matching plush robe. It was way too intimate to wear in front of her fake husband, even though he happened to be her real boyfriend now.

Come on, Iris. Help a girl out here. On a whim, she opened the door next to the credenza and discovered a massive walk-in closet with hanging bars and dozens of drawers and cubbies. It also contained a jewelry cabinet that lit up when she opened it, an ornate floor-to-ceiling mirror, and a bench of creamy soft leather.

On one of the bars hung the other cocktail dress of royal blue, a zany zebra stripe jumpsuit of pure silk, and a pink poodle skirt outfit with a note pinned to it.

In case you get selected to participate in the Grease skit.

Serena sure hoped that wouldn't be the case! She was already playing the role of a fake bride, thank you very much. Shuddering, she reached for the zebra-striped pantsuit. It was kind of atrocious, but she had no better options. She would simply have to make do with zebra stripes during her game planning session with Ransom.

Realizing she'd dawdled away nearly half of their agreed-upon changing time, she hastily opened the only other door in the room, hoping it was the bathroom. It was.

It contained a walk-in shower as big as a car wash, plus an elegant claw-foot tub. The marble vanity across from them boasted a stool topped with a white fur cushion. *Fur!* She bit back a chuckle at how over-the-top the furnishings were. Opting to take a quick dip in the tub, she turned on the tap water and adjusted the knobs to the perfect temperature.

Sorry, Ransom. I might take a little more than that half hour we agreed on. It was entirely his fault for setting her up in such luxurious accommodations. Though the steamy water felt amazing on her sore and tired feet, she resisted the temptation to soak. Despite her efforts to hurry, she knew she was pushing it on time to bathe and dress.

Her hair didn't get much more than a finger comb after she unpinned, but there was no way she was leaving the room without a quick dash of mascara and lip gloss. Then came the footwear decision. Since Iris had only packed stilettos in addition to her running shoes, she chose to remain barefoot.

By the time she returned to the lounge, Ransom was setting out a tray of finger foods. He glanced over his shoulder and straightened as she approached. "Hey, you."

"Hey." She hoped she didn't sound as nervous as she felt. A quick perusal of the tray revealed an array of meats, cheeses, crackers, olives, and dips. Despite the butterflies fluttering inside it, her stomach lurched with hunger pains. She hadn't eaten all day.

He waved at a stack of small white hors d'oeuvre plates. "Help yourself. I had no idea if you ate dinner before I picked you up this evening, so I ordered room service."

"Thank you. I'm famished." She reached for a plate, while eyeing his appearance from beneath her lashes. He was wearing distressed jeans and a short-sleeve navy t-shirt that hugged his upper arms and chest. Like her, he was barefoot.

She knew she was staring, but she couldn't help it. No way around it, her new boyfriend was a thousand shades of swoony.

"I take it Iris didn't pack you any jeans?" He took a seat on the sofa and leaned back to give her jumpsuit an amused once-over.

"Apparently, I fake married a genius," she noted dryly.

He chuckled and patted the seat next to him. "One of us did, anyway."

She remained acutely aware of every move he made and every breath he took as she accepted the plate he handed her. Because of how hungry she was, she didn't bother with modesty when it came to piling on the food.

To her surprise, he didn't grab a plate for himself. Instead, he ate off of hers, popping grapes and cheese cubes into his mouth and washing them down with a flute of sparkling water.

"Mmm." She briefly closed her eyes while sipping her berry-flavored water. "Everything is delicious. Thank you."

"Welcome." He unconsciously kneaded his left knee.

Her heart twisted with concern. "It's hurting again, isn't it?"

He glanced up at her and snorted. "It always hurts. If you want to distract me from the pain, I have a few ideas."

"Boom! You didn't hesitate to slap down the sympathy card." She set her empty plate on the coffee table in front of them and took another satisfying sip of her sparkling water.

He arched his dark eyebrows at her. "Is it working?"

"Yes," she assured softly, leaning closer.

"Then it was the right play." He turned his head to brush his lips against hers. "Yep. I feel better already." Making no move to take her in his arms, he gently dragged his mouth against hers a second time.

Since they'd set some pretty clear boundaries earlier, she leaned trustingly into the magic of his kisses. When he raised his head from hers, she murmured, "Thank you for the roses." She tipped her head against his shoulder as she awaited his reply.

"You're welcome." He reached up to trace the line of her cheek.

Her insides melted at the gentleness of his touch. "You went to a lot of effort to plan this weekend. More than you had to."

To her disappointment, he dropped his hand.

"Call me crazy, but I guess I was doing the things I wanted to do for the wife I don't have."

"It's not crazy." She instinctively understood what he was trying to say. Like her, he'd been longing for someone to love, so he'd been going through the motions.

"It kind of is," he muttered. "Considering the fact I'd more or less given up on ever finding someone like you."

"I'm flattered, but why give up?" The hopeless romantic side of her would never allow her to give up on love.

He shrugged, making her head move against his shoulder. "After you've prayed for something to happen for over twenty years, and crickets..."

"You prayed for a wife?" Golly, but she was digging the old-fashioned side of him!

"I did. Probably a few hundred times. After I lost my parents three years ago, I was left rattling around a too big, too quiet house."

"I'm sorry for your loss." Words never seemed adequate in situations like these.

"Thanks." His voice was low and rumbly in her ear.

"Mind if I ask what happened?" She hoped he didn't consider her curiosity too intrusive. However, if they were going to build a convincing back story about how they'd become a couple, it would help for her to know both the good and bad highlights of his life before her.

"Not at all. Can't think of too many things I'd mind telling my wife."

She smiled against his shoulder. "We don't have to keep playing our roles now that we're alone."

"It's good practice for the real thing, though, don't you think?"

"True." She caught her lower lip between her teeth, not able to come up with a witty comeback.

"It was a helicopter accident. I lost both of my parents at the same time."

"I'm so sorry, Ransom!"

He slid an arm around her shoulders, hugging her close. "Another kiss might help."

She chuckled. "That seems to be your fall-back remedy for everything."

He pressed his lips to her forehead. "Now that I've met you, it is."

She tipped her face up to his, and his mouth found hers. It was a long time before either of them spoke again.

"You make me happy, Serena." He toyed with a strand of her hair, wrapping it around his finger and giving it a gentle yank.

"Maybe you'll sleep it off," she teased.

"I doubt that, darlin'."

She tipped her head against his shoulder once again, content to simply be with him. "Aren't we supposed to be plotting what lies we're going to tell your friends tomorrow?"

"Or we could keep things simple and just tell the truth," he suggested quietly.

"Like the part about how we're not married?"

"Nah, I'd kinda like to keep that fib afloat a little longer. At least for the weekend."

"Me, too. If only to help put Macy Parker in her place."

"Is that fake jealously or the real deal?"

"A little of both, I'm afraid."

"You have nothing to worry about with her. Trust me."

"Maybe not right at this moment, but what if she makes a play for you tomorrow?"

"I don't think she's going to. No outsiders are allowed at Camden Hall reunions, so she had to come as a plus one to a grad. I'm starting to think Tucker might be her date. He was unusually testy with me earlier, for no apparent reason. Then again, it's been years since we last saw each other, and he was always hard to read."

She frowned, not able to get the details to add up inside her head. "Maybe, but I think it's more than that. If they were together, he'd have no reason to snipe at you the way he did — especially after he found out that you and I were married." She traced the hem of one of his shirt sleeves.

"You may have a point." He reached for her hand and held it captive against his heart.

"I know I do. I'm accustomed to compiling large amounts of marketing data and drawing conclusions."

"So what's your theory, Biostatistician Serena?"

"Well, assuming Tucker is truly part of the picture, I'd say that her attendance as his plus one might've simply been her ticket in the door. You're her real mark, though, and I think he knows it. The reason he's testy about it is because his affections are involved. Which would additionally explain her not-so-sunny reception of us at the welcome table. She probably wasn't expecting you to show up tonight with a wife."

He nodded, looking troubled. "Though your theory has merit, please don't be offended when I say what I'm about to say. I hope you're wrong."

"I hope I'm wrong, too." She relaxed, convinced at last that he had no intention of stirring any old embers with his high school sweetheart. "Now how about we get back to making up a few convincing fibs about how you and I met?"

CHAPTER 6: TOO HOT TO HANDLE
RANSOM

Ransom laid awake most of the night, pondering Serena's theory. The idea that members of the Pack might be conspiring to help Macy get back together with him felt like a betrayal. The Pack was supposed to be loyal to each other first, above all outsiders. If that pivotal commitment had changed, then the Pack was no more.

As for the thought of Macy Parker trying to get back with him? *Not happening!* She was yesterday's news. She'd had her chance with him, and she'd blown it, claiming she wasn't cut out for life as a soldier's wife. Her words had shattered any hope of a future between them. There was no coming back from a rejection like that. As lonely as he'd been during the past twenty years, he'd not once dreamed of getting back with the woman who wasn't able to accept him for who he was in the various roles God had called him to fill. Things were truly over between them. The sooner she and the Pack accepted that, the better for them all.

It had taken him a long time to find someone to fill that void in his life, but he was moving on with Serena. He smiled up at the ceiling. She was *the one*. He was sure of it. After spending his entire adult life scoffing at the idea of love at first sight, he'd fallen for her in a matter of minutes.

She was a game changer. All his fears about missing out on having a family due to his career choices were quickly fading beneath the happiness and hope she brought to the table. His gut told him that if things were meant to be between them, she would find a way to make it happen. She possessed an inner light and resilience he didn't often see in others. He was confident she could handle the challenges of being married to an ex soldier and fire rescue worker.

Maybe it was cocky of him to think in such terms, selfish even, but he was kind of glad she was poor. Maybe it would give him a small advantage when it came to sweeping her off her feet and riding with her into the sunset. Then again, she seemed to have a pretty solid moral compass. The fact that she'd tried to refuse payment for her Rent-A-Date contract was proof of that. On second thought, her humble bank account probably wasn't going to give him any advantage in pursuing her.

He was going to have to fall back on good, old-fashioned romance. He was going to have to compose poems and order flowers. He was going to have to worry and sweat about his chances of winning her heart like every other guy who dared to fall in love.

And she'd be worth every second of the chase. He rolled to the side of the bed, imagining what it would be like and feel like to have someone like her to hold, kiss, and cherish. And maybe — just maybe — start a family with some day.

Yeah, he was pushing the upside of thirty, but lots of guys became fathers at his age. The very idea of coming home every evening to Serena and their child instead of his big, empty house literally took his breath away. It would be like having every dream of his coming true at the same time.

Hanging on to that thought, he finally drifted off to sleep.

THE NEXT MORNING, he stepped into the lounge in his running shorts and sneakers to discover Serena had beat him to the coffee maker. Two freshly brewed mugs were steaming on the side bar. She glanced up at him from the area rug, where she was bent forward, touching her toes.

"Morning, Sleeping Beauty," she teased, nodding in the direction of the coffee. "It's a hazelnut and vanilla blend. Wasn't sure what your favorite poison was." She crossed her legs and bent to touch her toes again. He watched in amazement as she flattened her palms all the way against the floor. Now *that* was limber!

He stepped farther into the room, drinking in the sight of her crazy long blonde ponytail and toned runner's legs. No way around it, his new girlfriend was smoking hot!

She was wearing a pair of black silk running shorts and a sleeveless pink shirt. Her well-defined upper arms indicated she was no stranger to the gym. Since maintaining his physical fitness had always been an important part of the jobs he worked, he easily recognized the signs.

He passed up the coffee bar to join her on the rug. Standing next to her, he stretched — not quite able to reach his toes the way she'd so easily done. "I'm going to let you in on a little secret. You're my favorite poison, Serena Chandler."

"Oo, points for Romeo!" He was pretty sure the blush staining her cheeks had nothing to do with the fact she was bent over double.

"Want to join me for a few couples' stretches?" He straightened and reached for her hand.

Her blue gaze sharpened with intrigue. "Couples stretches? Is that what the kids are calling it these days?"

"Get over here, and I'll show you." When she

placed her hand in his, he tugged her to the floor with him. "Stretch your legs out in front of you," he instructed, moving to sit directly across from her. He mirrored her movements, touching the bottom of his sneakers to hers. "Now give me your hands."

"Oh, I see what you have in mind! I haven't done these since my cheerleading days," she squealed, reaching eagerly for him.

A cheerleader, eh? A few more details about her clicked into place. Her athleticism, charisma, and beauty certainly fit that package. "Competitive or recreational?" he inquired with raised eyebrows.

"Both." Her voice was a little muffled, since her face was pressed all the way to her knees. "I earned my undergrad degree on a cheerleading scholarship."

Which additionally meant she'd been a really talented cheerleader. "Congratulations!" He slowly pulled her hands past her toes and was amazed when their joined hands reached his ankles. Afraid of hurting her, he stopped.

"Go a little more," she urged.

He slowly tugged her another inch in his direction.

"Okay. That's good," she gasped.

He just as slowly eased their joined hands back to her toes. "My turn."

She raised her head and nodded, tugging his hands in return until she made him grunt against the ache of resistance he encountered.

Her gaze landed on the puckered scars above his bare knees. "How long were you in therapy for your injuries?"

"Months." It was actually closer to a year, but he didn't like talking about it.

"Wrong answer," she informed him flatly.

"Oh?" He shot her a curious look.

"With injuries like that, you'll always be in therapy," she chided. "That is, if you have any interest in living pain free."

"I'm listening." He shot her a wistful look. If there was any chance in the universe of living pain free, he'd jump all over it.

"It was killing you last night, wasn't it?" She curled forward to balance on her knees.

He shrugged. "The dancing helped loosen it up. The woman I was dancing with was a pretty great distraction, too."

"May I?" She splayed her hands in the air above his knee, waiting for his permission to touch.

"Be my guest." *I'm all yours, darlin'.*

Flushing, she gently kneaded the muscle tissue around his old injury, making adjustments to her movements each time he winced. "These muscle straps are so tight, it's no wonder your leg was killing you all evening. You should be stretching them out every day. Several times per day, in fact."

She put him through a pretty thorough routine that included pressing his knee all the way to his chest, then straightening out his leg and pushing it as far past the bend as he could bear.

Her touch was like magic. He was amazed at how much better his knee felt afterward. "Did you learn all this in cheerleading?" He rolled forward to rest his forearms on his knees, keeping her hands loosely clasped in his. It appeared that their stretching session was over, but he was nowhere near ready to let her go.

"I guess you could say that. I suffered a small tear to my ACL a few years ago that thankfully didn't require surgery. It earned me several months in therapy, though. The therapist I was assigned to insisted that I needed to maintain everything he was teaching me for life. Otherwise, my mobility might digress at whatever point I stopped."

"So you didn't stop."

"And I'm never going to." She smiled. "He made a believer out of me. Under his coaching, I became a lifelong fitness guru and health nut. Add that to my natural flare for nerdiness, and—"

"You're an incredible person, Serena Chandler." And utterly perfect for him. Though it was rude to interrupt her, he didn't like the way she tended to put herself down so often. "Anyone who has ever made you feel differently is dead wrong." Feeling inspired, he kicked off his shoes.

Her lips parted on a gasp as he tugged her hands back over his knees and slowly rolled with her to his back, lifting her over his head with his feet and their joined hands.

She gave a squeal of excitement as she figured out what he was doing. "You're crazy," she panted as her ponytail swung down between them. "You know that, right?"

"Crazy for you, maybe." He blew her a kiss. "Show me something cool you learned in cheerleading. That's my price for letting you come back down."

"Hmm. Okay." She arched her lower back and stretched her legs out behind her. Then she let one of his hands go and reached back to pull one leg over her head into a perfect scorpion pose.

"You're so beautiful," he whispered. He waited until she returned to their original position. Then he slowly lowered her towards him until their lips touched.

Then he allowed her to use his arms for leverage until her feet returned to the floor.

She was blushing when she reached back to help pull him to his feet beside her. "You're full of surprises, Sergeant Keller."

"You're welcome." Grinning, he swooped in for another quick kiss. "I hate to break it to you, but it's time to go check in at the park now. I think we missed coffee hour."

She didn't look overly concerned. "It still counts as my turn. You get to brew the next batch."

"Duly noted, Mrs. Keller." His heartbeat sped at the thought of making her coffee — not just the time during their short first weekend together, but again and again for the rest of their lives, Lord willing. He bent to tug his tennis shoes back on. For now, though, it was time to focus on his high school reunion again.

"Quick review of the back story we invented last night." The soldier in him liked to be clear on his marching orders before stepping into battle. "We met at a Veteran's appreciation gig at the university on the Fourth of July. It was love at first sight, and we eloped to a resort in Corpus Christi a few weeks later." To the beach house he conveniently owned and had every intention of inviting her to come visit soon. "Our reasons for keeping the ceremony short, sweet, and private are anchored loosely in the loss of both sets of parents. I doubt anyone is going to want to pick that story apart."

"Yes. We're turning out to be pretty convincing liars." Serena smirked. "And the fact that we've known each other for less than two months, during which I've continued to attend college full time, will hopefully explain any holes in our stories."

"We'll tell the truth about everything else, and nothing but the truth, so help us God." He raised his right hand to mimic the swearing in part of a court hearing. "My prediction is that no one will guess that we've actually known each other much less than the stated two months."

She high-fived him. "I think that covers it. We've already gone over all the basics. Favorite colors, foods, and movies. We're seriously about as studied up as I get for my final exams."

He held out his arms to her. "I could use another kiss to fortify me against what's coming." Though he'd agreed to play Truth Or Dare with a group of nosy pranksters and a spiteful ex-girlfriend, he wasn't looking forward to it. He would have much rather spent the afternoon alone with Serena.

She stepped into his embrace and slid her arms around his neck. "We've got this." She touched her lips to his.

One kiss led to another one. They nearly missed the beginning of the race, which earned them plenty of ragging from the Pack.

"Newlyweds!" Matt shook his head in derision when they jogged up to the starting line. "Way to keep rubbing it in!"

It was a balmy, seventy-degree morning with a light breeze in play. The main running path at the park had been roped off and reserved for the event. Road guards in neon yellow vests were posted at water stations and key locations along the way. Most importantly, the tickets were sold out. The funds would provide some much-needed assistance with the medical expenses of a classmate fighting a rare lung disease.

Dash-for-Asher banners and posters were

displayed at the starting line and at the tables being set up for the picnic brunch afterwards. Ransom thought it was very appropriate that their student council had decided to use their class reunion as an opportunity to support Asher and his family. He was glad to be a part of such a worthy cause.

He was doubly glad to be a part of such a cause with the gorgeous Serena Chandler at his side. His fake bride extraordinaire. His very real girlfriend. His personal gift from heaven.

She was bouncing on her toes and doing leg lifts to keep her muscles warmed up, a routine that earned her no small number of admiring male glances.

And a few envious female ones.

A cluster of his classmates' wives were standing on the sidelines with children of various ages. Disposable paper pom-poms were being distributed to the kids, which meant they would be serving as the school's unofficial cheering squad during the race.

All of Ransom's classmates were participating in the charity run, even a classmate in a wheelchair. Another classmate limped forward, wearing a leg brace. It was a Camden Hall tradition to include everyone in their spirit runs. Those who couldn't run were welcome to walk or ride the course. It was a tradition that Ransom was enormously proud to be a part of.

Macy glanced up from her position at the front of the line and shot a withering look at his and Serena's joined hands. He nodded at her, not letting his gaze linger too long on her barely-there running shorts and tank top that left her midriff bare. Her outfit might appeal to some guys, but he didn't find it nearly as attractive as what Serena had on. Sometimes it was best to leave a little to the imagination.

For the life of him, he couldn't recall Macy showing that much skin in the past. She'd clearly changed, and not in a good way. Though she was still a relatively attractive woman, she came across as bitter and, quite frankly, a little desperate. It made him wonder what kind of marriage she'd gotten herself tangled up in — not a good one, apparently, since it hadn't lasted. Not that it was his problem to worry about, but things like that could explain a lot.

"On your mark." The announcer raised his cap gun. "Get set. Goooooo!" He shot into the air, and the runner's took off.

Macy and Tucker took the early lead, sprinting for all they were worth to put distance between them and the other runners. Once in front, however, they settled into a more maintainable speed.

Exchanging a mischievous look with Serena, Ransom deliberately paced the two top competitors. If it was a stock car race, his maneuver would have been called back drafting. Though wind currents didn't play near as big of a role with runners, he figured what he was doing would wear on Macy's nerves.

It didn't take long for her and Tucker to figure out they didn't have the win in the bag. They tried to keep their edge with a few short sprints, but all Ransom and Serena had to do was notch up their steady pace, and they soon caught up.

There was no way Serena was giving the race all she had, since she wasn't even close to becoming winded. He knew this because she hadn't stopped breathing through her nose. She was a very disciplined runner, focusing on her stride and breathing instead of focusing on the pair in front of them. It dawned on him in slow degrees that she was actually a viable candidate for taking first place.

Tucker was visibly wearing down by the second mile, which earned him several irritated glances from his running partner. He finally tapped her lightly on the shoulder and conceded defeat by falling back at the beginning of the third mile. If Ransom had to venture a guess, it was the sprints that had done him in. Most folks simply weren't in that kind of shape at their age.

"She's going to leave you in her dust," Tucker panted as Ransom and Serena overtook him. "You don't stand a chance."

Yeah, the Pack was dead. Ransom's heart lurched in disappointment, but he didn't give his friend the satisfaction of a response. All it would have done was eat up valuable air and energy.

He maintained his silence until they rounded the final bend and had the finish line in sight. It was a good fifty meters or so away, plenty of time to change the outcome of a race.

Then he leaned closer to Serena. "You got this, darlin'. Let her rip."

She glanced up in surprise. That was when he realized she'd not intended to win the race. "Are you sure?"

He nodded and started clapping and yelling, "Go, Serena! Go!"

She kicked it in gear with such an impressive burst of speed that all he could do for a few seconds was gaze, star-struck, after her. Then he resumed his cheering.

Serena whizzed past Macy, her long slender legs pumping like a gazelle. She was grace and beauty in motion. Complete perfection. And she was his.

She crossed the finish line several strides ahead of Macy. Only because Macy seemed to lose heart and slowed down at the end instead of sprinting across the finish line, Ransom was able to catch up with her. They crossed at the same time, and the time keeper announced it was a tie for second place.

The main party of runners, including the rest of the Pack, joined the revelers at the finish line over the next thirty seconds or so. Bellowing in triumph,

Ransom hoisted Serena to his shoulders and paraded around the winner's circle with her. A cameraman snapped picture after picture of them.

The Pack converged on them, and they posed for a Pack photo while jointly holding up Serena sideways.

Afterward, Ransom swung her in another circle before setting her back on her feet and sealing his mouth over hers.

What had started out as an elaborate prank, in bringing a fake bride to his high school reunion, had backfired in the most joyous of ways. He vowed right then and there that his mother's wedding ring was never coming off Serena's finger. He was going to do whatever it took to convince her to keep it on.

For good.

CHAPTER 7: TRUTH OR DARE

RANSOM

"That was so much fun," Serena exclaimed on their walk back to the hotel.

Not caring that they were both blasting sweat bombs, he looped an arm around her slender waist and hugged her as they passed through the revolving glass doors at the front entrance. "You were awesome out there. I was so proud of your win that I almost started blubbering like a baby."

"Speaking of babies," she rolled her eyes, "winning the race felt a little too much like stealing candy from one."

"Hey!" He scowled down at her. "You were the strongest runner out there. It was a fair race and a justifiable win."

Her lush lips turned down at the corners. "Maybe, but the race meant a lot more to Macy than it did to me. Part of me feels really bad for her right now."

Only because you're one of the sweetest, kindest people who has ever walked the face of this miserable planet! "Trust me, darlin', her reasons were far from noble."

"Are you sure about that, Ransom?" She raised her troubled gaze to his. "Because, if truly she came to this reunion with plans to try to win you back, I can't exactly criticize her taste in men."

"Thank you." His voice was cautious since he had no idea what point she was leading up to.

"You're welcome. All I'm saying is, I'm having a hard time villainizing her over the fact that she might have finally woken up and realized what an amazing guy she gave up years ago."

"It's too late, Serena." He slapped the up button of the elevator controls, hardly believing they were having this conversation. "That train has long since left the station. It's over between us — no if's, and's, or but's about it."

"Of course it's over, you nut." She waited until the elevator doors rolled shut behind them before looping her arms around his neck. "We're married, remember?" She stood on her tiptoes to brush her mouth against his. "At least for one more day."

He devoured her lips, still euphoric about her taking first place at the charity run. "Just for the record, I have no plans of giving you up." He punctuated his vow with another very thorough kiss. "Ever!"

Her smile was tremulous. "In case you're wondering, I'm in no terrible hurry for this weekend to end, either."

The elevator stopped on the top floor, but he remained standing there with her cuddled in his embrace for another moment.

A breathy chuckle eased out of her. "Unless you want to have the smelliest girlfriend at the next event, we should probably go shower."

Right. He reluctantly dropped his arms to dig in his pocket for the elevator key.

When the elevator door slid open, she backed into their penthouse suite, still talking. "The whole time we were running, I was brainstorming our plan of action for the Truth Or Dare game."

He followed her. "Oh, really?"

"I came up with a few super good ideas that I can't wait to share with you." She kicked off her sneakers and left them sitting against the wall by the elevator.

He did the same. "I can't wait to hear them."

"Showers first. Then we'll have our new powwow." She danced down the hallway and disappeared from sight.

He stared after her, thoroughly entranced. After he showered, he started to change into jeans and a t-shirt. Recalling that Serena had brought no casual attire with her, however, he upgraded his outfit to a white button-up shirt and beige slacks. He toned it down a few degrees by rolling up his sleeves and stepping into a pair of leather loafers.

Serena joined him in the lounge, wearing a mouth-watering dress in a shade of blue that made her eyes look almost purple. She gave a quick twirl for his benefit that made the full skirt fan out at her knees. It also gave him a glimpse of the large criss-cross straps that spanned her sun-kissed shoulders.

"You look amazing." His heart pounded in anticipation of getting to show her off again to his friends.

"Thanks."

He glanced down at her feet. "Going barefoot again?"

She wrinkled her nose at him. "Don't I wish! I'm just waiting as long as I can before making my choice between the stilettos or stilettos that Iris was kind enough to pack for me."

He shrugged. "Or your sneakers," he reminded with a grin.

She blew her bangs off her forehead. "And commit fashion suicide? Iris would shoot me if she found out. I'm still on the clock, remember?"

He preferred to forget that dismal point, hating that their relationship had begun with such a mercenary transaction. *Oh, well.* The most important thing was that they *had* met.

"As I was saying earlier, I had this brainstorm during our run." Serena plopped down on one of the sofas as she slid on a pair of tan peep-toe pumps — the stilts version.

"Lay it on me." He raised his eyebrows at her.

"I should probably backtrack a second to build my case."

"Okay." She sounded so serious that he inwardly braced himself.

"I've never met Tucker before, so maybe he's always been a bit of a bozo, but my gut tells me his testiness has everything to do with his secret crush on Macy."

"A theory you laid out rather eloquently yesterday." Though he inclined his head to share his agreement, he honestly couldn't have cared less about Macy's love life. Or Tucker's. Or anyone else's, for that matter. Couldn't Serena see that? His focus was one hundred percent on her — his lovely fake bride that he had every intention of making his real bride as soon as possible. Yeah, it was a bit sudden to be leaping forward with thoughts in that direction, but he couldn't help it. He'd waited so long to meet someone like her. Every second he spent in her presence made him all the more sure that they were heading towards happily-ever-after.

"So you agree there might be something going on between Macy and Tucker? Something, I might add, that she might not even be able to see, since her radar is so set on you right now."

"It's possible." He spread his hands. "What are you getting at, darlin'?" He lowered his arms back to his sides, hoping she'd spit it out as plainly as possible.

"I'm glad you asked." Her smile turned wicked. "Here's my brainstorm. I think we should turn the tables on Macy and Tucker. Let's beat them at their own game of Truth Or Dare."

His gazed narrowed with interest on hers, liking the sound of that immensely. "What exactly do you have in mind, Mrs. Keller?"

She folded her slender arms. "During the game, we should bait Tucker big-time with the kind of questions that might lead up to a confession of his feelings."

He snickered. Oh, this was good! "What about Macy?"

"We should go the dare route with her. Try to maneuver her and Tucker into some sort of romantic overture. A kiss. A hug. A shoulder rub. I don't know. Something to redirect her focus on him."

"That's diabolical!" He shook a finger at her. "Remind me to never get on your bad side."

"Never get on my bad side, Sergeant Keller," she taunted, rising to her feet and gliding in his direction on her impossibly high heels. "Do you have any objections to my plan? Any old feelings that might interfere with our chance of success?"

He waited until she was standing directly in front of him before stooping to speak directly against her ear. "If you have any doubts whatsoever about where I stand on the issue, I haven't kissed you near enough this weekend."

She gave a satisfied little sigh that made his heart ache with happiness.

"Now that we've squared that away," he straightened, "I'm as happy as a bronc without a bucking strap that we've decided to go on the offensive here."

While she was chuckling at his choice of words, he strode across the room to grab his Stetson from the hall tree.

On their way down in the elevator, he kept an arm slung around her shoulders, enjoying her nearness. And craving it, too. After years of being single, it was really nice having someone to share his life with. He hoped she didn't mind his show of possessiveness. The way he saw it, though, a guy couldn't be too careful in a conference center teaming with rich and successful alumni from an all-male prep school.

Especially the guy fortunate enough to have the loveliest plus one in all of Dallas at his side.

Serena's eyes widened in surprise and pleasure to find Jarvis waiting for them at the curb with his black limo. "Did you reserve him for the whole weekend or what?"

"Yes." Ransom nodded a hello to Jarvis as he opened the passenger door for them.

He tipped his visor at them. "How's the reunion going, soldier?"

Ransom gestured at Serena. "You have to ask?"

Jarvis looked confused. Ransom bent closer to inform him in an undertone before he climbed inside the vehicle. "We're dating now. For real."

"Congratulations!" Jarvis's expression was warm with approval as he shut the door behind them.

"What was that all about?" Serena glanced over her shoulder at their driver as he rounded the front of the vehicle and returned to the driver's seat.

Ransom reached for her hand and settled back against the plush leather cushions. "I think he's rooting for us."

"So am I," she informed him softly.

He raised her hand to his lips. "Me, too, and I'm liking our odds, darlin'."

It was a short drive to the high school's oldest gym facility, where Ransom discovered — to his complete lack of surprise — that he and Serena were overdressed. The other guys were in jeans or board shorts. Remy's pregnant wife was in a voluminous sundress and flip-flops, and Macy was wearing a pair of too-short jean shorts. *Shocker...not!*

A volleyball net was set up in the center of the room. Owen and Matt were bumping a ball back and forth over it. The original wooden floor was heavily scuffed with age, but it was shined to a full gloss. The bleachers on both sides of the room were rolled closed against the walls, and the basketball nets were missing from their rims. The state championship flags and MVP posters had long since been removed and relocated to the new gym on the other side of campus, but Ransom could still picture how they'd once looked, displayed in all their glory around the perimeter of the room.

"What part about a gym party didn't you understand, bro?" Tucker's tone was snide as he leaned in to clap him on the back.

Ransom was half-tempted to collect Serena right then and there and leave the event. However, out of the corner of his eye, he noted her kicking off her heels and making a beeline for the court. "This should be interesting." Chuckling, he folded his arms and prepared to be entertained.

Tucker stepped back, scowling at him. "I don't get it," he growled. "It's like she came out of nowhere."

Ransom raised his eyebrows at him, pretending innocence. "Who? Macy?"

Tucker snorted. "I think we both know I was referring to Serena. Why haven't the rest of us gotten to meet her before now? We're supposed to be the Pack. Brothers for life."

Ransom's smile slipped. "The Pack is dead," he returned coldly. "It died the moment I arrived at the welcome desk to find my ex had been invited by our class president. A guy who was supposed to be one of my best friends."

Tucker glanced away, an agonized expression twisting his features.

"She's your plus one, isn't she?" he snarled. Not that he minded that in itself. It was the duplicity he objected to.

Tucker hung his head. "It's not what you think, Keller."

Ransom's heart sank to realize that everything Serena suspected about his friend was probably true. The fact that the guy was harboring a crush on a woman he didn't stand a chance with meant he was in for some real heartache in the coming days. Sadly, Ransom didn't share Serena's optimism about redirecting Macy's focus to Tucker. Macy was like a hound with a bloody bone once she made up her mind she wanted something — stubborn and heartless in her pursuit of it.

Not my problem anymore. He was truly grateful to have dodged that particular bullet. "I don't really care what the two of you have going on, or not going on, between you. What matters to me is Serena. You gotta problem with her, you gotta problem with me."

Tucker threw his arms up in surrender, backing away and looking thoroughly chastised. "I don't have a problem with either of you, and the Pack isn't dead. And you're right about Macy. I did agreed to lend her a hand this weekend, but only because I thought it would be a cool thing to do, since you never married and she's single again. In my defense," he held up a finger, "that was before I had any idea you'd gotten married. That's on you, bro, for failing to inform us about something that important. That said, if you'll give me half a chance, I'll find a way to fix this."

Ransom gave him a hard, searching look, then nodded. "Half a chance. For old time's sake."

Tucker nodded back. "You still should have told us about Serena. No matter how many years have passed since high school, not getting invited to your wedding is just plain wrong, man."

"Maybe you're right." Ransom inclined his head in apology, experiencing a burst of guilt over his own duplicity. He glanced across the room in time to catch Owen high-fiving Serena. It warmed his heart to witness how accepting of her the other Pack members were being. Maybe Tucker was right about them, too. Maybe the Pack wasn't dead, after all.

"You know I'm right, bro." With a huff of regret, Tucker moved across the room to check on the food line. Caterers in white aprons were setting up a row of silver warming trays.

Ransom gave the air a sniff of appreciation. Unless he was mistaken, Tucker had ordered food from their favorite high school hangout, the Downtown Diner. Years ago, their classmates had fondly renamed it the Double D Corral. His mouth watered at the memories of their chicken-fried steak, barbecued ribs, and sweet corn casserole. Their hand-mixed shakes and fountain sodas weren't too shabby, either.

It was a little warm in the room, probably from all the gas burners glowing beneath the serving pans, but it was worth the rise in temperature to sample the diner's food again after all these years. They could always cool down after lunch with an ice cream shake.

Tucker unearthed a megaphone and held it to his mouth. "Alright, alright, alright! The twentieth reunion of The Camden Hall one and only Pack is officially called to order." He pretended to pound a gavel. "No, seriously, y'all. It's really great to have the gang back together again today. It doesn't happen near enough these days, and I plan to change that. Life's too short and blah blah blah. Anyhow, before Owen starts another flash mob dance to shut me up, I'll just say this." He paused a beat. "Let's eat!"

Everyone crowded eagerly around the food table, which soon turned into a scuffle between Matt and Owen as to who would get the first scoop of corn casserole. Their bickering made it feel just like old times.

Serena padded barefoot up to Ransom with her ponytail askew and eyes shining. "Your friends are pretty great guys."

"Yeah." He slung an arm around her shoulders. "They are."

She leaned into him. "I know there have been some tough things about this weekend, but you don't have to let it come between you and the Pack."

He snorted. "Tucker said nearly the same thing to me a few minutes ago."

"Tucker, huh? That's not the guy I would've expected to hear that from."

"No kidding!" He momentarily cuddled her closer.

They joined the food line and filled their plates, then joined the others at a banquet table set up not too far from the serving line.

Owen leaned forward on his elbows and spoke with his mouth full. "We should start the Truth Or Dare game now."

Jenn and Macy burst out laughing at his muffled announcement.

He finished chewing and swallowed. "It would leave us more time for volleyball. Just saying."

Tucker glanced in Ransom's direction. "Or we could just skip it altogether. We're not fifteen anymore."

Ransom nodded, greatly gratified, but Macy leaned forward with a pout. "Oh, come on! This is the Pack we're talking about! Since when did y'all turn into a bunch of old party poopers?"

Owen balanced his fork on his nose and stood without dropping it. "Since never!" he crowed, flipping the fork from his nose. It flew across the room. "Let's get this party started." He made a stirring motion with both hands. "I hereby volunteer to go first."

"Fine, but only after you hear the modified Pack rules of engagement." Macy held up one red-tipped finger. "There will be three rounds, during which everyone will get one turn apiece." She held up a second finger. "Only one skipped turn per person will be permitted. Think of it as a lifeline." A third finger went up. "There will be no pile of pre-written questions or dares. Whoever's turn it is can ask any question or make any dare they choose, so long as it doesn't endanger the health or safety of others."

Tucker waved two fingers in the air. "And as your beloved president, I reserve the right to strike any question or dare off the table to keep things fun."

"Since when?" Macy sounded disappointed.

"Are you questioning the leader of the Pack?" His tone was teasing, but his expression indicated the item was a non-negotiable.

She sank back into her seat, arms crossed in irritation. However, she didn't argue the point further.

"Alright, Owen." Tucker cocked his thumb and forefinger at his friend. "You're up."

"Roger that!" Owen tapped his fingers together and issued an evil cackle as he gazed around the table. "Who will be my first victim?" His gaze landed on Serena. "That would be you."

"Oh, yay." Her tone was playfully lackluster, eliciting a few chuckles.

"Truth or dare, beautiful?"

She drew a deep breath. "Truth, I guess."

He promptly marched around the table and took a knee before her. Clasping his hands dramatically, he cried, "Please, please, please assure me you have a hot, single sister!"

Everyone in the room, except Macy, dissolved into laughter.

"That's not a question." She turned to Tucker. "I think he should forfeit."

He treated her to a lordly stare. "Where's the fun in that?" He turned to Owen. "You get one chance to rephrase it as a question. If you've forgotten that much grammar since high school, then I'll have no choice but to grant Serena's request and have you forfeit."

Keeping his hands clasped, Owen hurriedly asked, "Do you have any hot sisters?"

She shook her head. "Sadly, I'm an only child."

"It's a cruel, cruel world." He stood, head dropping in defeat. "Speaking of hot, I don't think the

AC is working very well. Mind if I prop the doors open?"

"Oh, please do!" Matt's wife, Jenn, was furiously fanning her face. Fortunately, there was a nice Texas breeze blowing outside, which quickly returned the room to a more bearable temperature.

The game ended up being more fun than Ransom originally anticipated. Matt was dared to swallow a "red tornado," which was their teenage nickname for mixing every condiment on the table in a single glass. He managed to do it, then ran from the room clutching his stomach. He returned, looking better and guzzling a bottle of water. "I'm too old for that," he groaned. "I think I'll just tell the truth on the next round."

Remy was dared to don an old football jersey that his wife produced. The trick was, he had to do it standing on his hands with his feet propped against the gym wall. Which he did, after a few awkward and insanely hilarious contortions.

Ransom was the next victim. He raised his chin and met Tucker's questioning gaze, expecting the worst.

"Truth or dare?" Tucker asked in a low, silky voice.

"Dare." He figured performing a silly trick was a safer option than subjecting himself to an interrogation about his relationship with Serena.

"You sure about that?"

Ransom glanced around the table. Most of his friends were watching him with anticipatory smiles. Macy was staring down at her plate. "I'm sure."

"Alright, buddy. You walked into this one with your eyes wide open." He leaned forward. "I dare you to plant a kiss on the one female in the world you've had the longest running relationship with."

Macy's head came up in shock, and Serena looked a little sick. Everyone else at the table lost their smiles.

"Well, this is awkward." Ransom sat back in his seat, folding his arms as he watched the caterers pack away their meal. They packaged up the leftovers, then took turns carting out the empty silver trays, one by one. *One female, eh?* The wheels in his brain spun. While everyone else at the table was quietly freaking out, he decided to have a little fun with the fact that Tucker had failed to state he had to kiss a human female. He'd simply used the term *female*.

"You want to turn this one down, bro?" Tucker taunted.

Ransom grinned. "Not on your life. I just need to make a phone call first."

"What? To your divorce attorney?" Owen chortled.

Ransom stood. "A private phone call, if you don't mind. I don't believe there are any rules about disclosing our sources. Carry on with the game. I promise to return in a few minutes." He bent over

Serena and tipped up her chin to plant one on her. "I'll beg your forgiveness right now, publicly and with great humility."

"I'll consider it and give you my decision after the game," she teased.

"Fair enough." He tenderly brushed his lips against hers again, then left the room. Pulling out his cell phone, he dialed his chief at the firehouse.

"Axel Hammerstone speaking. What's your emergency?"

It took nearly a half hour for Axel to arrive in an unmarked emergency vehicle with his lights flashing. He leaped from the driver's seat in his fireproof uniform and steel-toed boots. A former Marine, he was impressively tall and broad.

"You owe me one." He slapped on his helmet and raised the rear door of the dark SUV to reveal an enormous cage. "Big time!"

"Just add it to my tab."

Ransom's search and rescue dog, Princess, barked happily at the sight of him. She was a tall, sleek Dalmatian, who'd served as his K9 partner for the past five years. Fortunately, Ransom had dated Macy Parker for only four years.

Axel shook his head in amusement. "I didn't know you even had a girlfriend."

"She's new."

His friends' eyebrows shot upward. "Clearly."

"For reasons I don't have time to go into at the

moment, everyone inside thinks she's my wife, and I'd like them to continue thinking that for a little longer."

Axel raised and lowered his massive shoulders. "I'm not touching that."

"Appreciate it. Can you wait here a few minutes with the cage?"

"So long as I don't get called to put out a fire. You know the drill."

"Fair enough." Ransom lightly punched his shoulder. "Like I said, I owe you." He unlatched Princess's cage and whistled for her to jump down to the ground. Then he gave her the motion to follow him. Since she was trained to attack on command, he kept her on a chain. It was with great pride that he re-entered the gym with his award-winning canine partner at his side.

At the sight of the two of them together, the merriment in the room grew hushed.

"You're back." Tucker looked surprised. Macy, on the other hand, looked crestfallen.

"Boys and girls, I'd like you to meet Princess." Ransom halted a safe distance from his table of friends and commanded the dog to sit. "I am greatly honored to have spent the past five years working with this brave and highly talented fire rescue partner. She and I first met at the Texas Hotline Training Center, where we spent a whole month working together. In the five years since then, she's run into countless burning buildings and saved countless lives." He glanced down at her, feeling a little emotional as he commanded her to stand. "You may or may not be able to see it from this distance, but one of her paws is permanently scarred from wounds sustained in action. She's a real hero, folks. That said, she'll probably bite my face off if I try to kiss her." He gave a dry laugh. "Rescue dogs aren't house pets. They're lethal weapons, which is why they're able to do what they have to do every day."

Tucker stood and started clapping. "I hereby veto the kiss and declare your turn served. There's no topping this one. Game over, folks!"

Their friends erupted into cheers.

Ransom sought out and held Serena's gaze. The glow of pride in her gaze made him feel ten feet tall.

A loud crackling sound made Princess growl and paw at the floor. The planks beneath them shifted ominously.

"Is it just me," one of the wives murmured, "or do I smell smoke?"

Ransom's brain raced at the possibilities. Hot, old building. Crackling sound. Smoke. Was it possible they'd mistaken a malfunctioning air conditioner for something else? The faint scent of sulfur was his final clue as to what was going on.

"The boiler room!" he shouted. "I think it's about to blow." He moved his hand in a violent circular motion to urge his friends toward the nearest exit. "We need to evacuate the building! Now!"

No sooner had his friends started running, the crackling sound turned into a whistling screech. Princess lurched into motion and followed him toward the front entrance of the building. Before they reached the doors, the floor behind them exploded.

CHAPTER 8: ONE LAST DARE
SERENA

The sound was so loud and horrifying that Serena instinctively dove to the floor, covering her head with her hands. The building shuddered and cracked as if it was trying to break in half. She heard Jenn scream and Macy sob out something, but she couldn't see much. Smoke billowed into the room, making them choke.

"Everyone, stay low!" Owen shouted. "Find something to cover your mouth and nose with." He low-crawled his way to Serena. "You okay?"

She squinted at him through eyes that were burning and streaming from the smoke. When she tried to answer him, the only thing that came out was a cough.

With a grimace, he shrugged out of his t-shirt and pressed it to her face.

She gratefully accepted it, and he moved on.

Because of the poor visibility in the room, it took a few minutes for everyone in their group to find their friends or loved ones. Tucker and Macy were the last to be located. He was unconscious, half sprawled across her.

"I'm afraid to move," she cried hoarsely. "Is he...is he—?" She couldn't seem to bring herself to ask the question.

Serena noted that she was clinging like a lifeline to Tucker's limp hand.

Owen leaped forward to check his pulse. "He's still with us," he shouted joyously. "We need to find a way out of here and get him to the hospital."

"I've already called 911." Remy was stooped over Jenn, who was clutching her belly. "I think my wife is having contractions."

They quickly came to the realization that leaving the building might not be as easy as they originally thought. The front exit was blocked by a wall of flames. The back exit was barricaded by a mountainous collection of old, discarded furniture — tables, chairs, desks, lamps, and floor-to-ceiling boxes. Everyone except Tucker and Jenn jumped up and started moving furniture as quickly as they could to dismantle the barricade.

Serena's hands shook as she worked. She had no idea what their chances were of clearing a path before the fire reached them. The grim expressions that the Pack members wore weren't encouraging. All the coughing and gagging around her made her additionally worry about how much time they had left before smoke inhalation became a problem.

Aside from their incessant coughing, they worked mostly in silence, reserving the bulk of their energy for moving furniture. As Serena dragged furniture from the pile, she tried to hold on to the hope that Ransom was out there somewhere behind the wall of flames. She instinctively knew that he was doing everything he could to reach them.

So long as he'd survived the explosion, himself.

Please, God. She mouthed the prayer over and over as she worked. *Please let him be alright. Help him reach us in time.*

After what felt like a million years, a fire engine wailed in the distance.

"You hear that, folks? Help is on the way!" Owen's voice was raspy from the smoke. "We just gotta hang on a little longer."

Everyone who could continued to toss aside furniture, feverishly trying to clear a path to the rear exit.

Another loud crackling sound rent the air. Serena paused in the act of lifting a chair to watch the roof slowly implode inward. Seconds later, arcs of water poured through the opening, drenching the room. The clouds of smoke that had been threatening to suffocate them, billowed upward through the opening in the ceiling, finding the release it craved. Almost immediately, she found it easier to breathe.

It might have been seconds later, minutes, or even an hour, but a tall, familiar figure strode through the smoke and flames. He made a beeline for her. "Serena?" he cried.

She stared in stunned fascination for a moment. Then her knees started to shake, threatening to crumble beneath her. She waffled between dizziness and relief to discover her fake husband was still alive.

"Ransom," she called weakly. Her legs finished giving out, and she slid to the floor.

RANSOM INSISTED that Serena pay a visit to the hospital, though she assured him again and again that she was fine. Tucker ended up being the only one seriously injured. During the explosion, he'd thrown himself on top of Macy and broken his leg. It was a clean break, though. He was going to be bound by a cast and crutches for a few weeks, but he was going to be fine.

Whether driven by guilt or some other emotion, Macy refused to leave his hospital room, even to eat. The other Pack members took turns delivering refreshments, changes of clothing, and other necessities.

No, the Pack wasn't dead as Ransom had feared. It was still very much alive, strengthened more than ever by the shared dangers they'd endured today.

Jenn was okay, too. Her contractions turned out to be false labor pains brought on by the suffocating heat, mild dehydration, and stress. She was admitted for observation as a precaution. However, she was hopeful of receiving a clean bill of health and discharge papers by morning.

A very bedraggled and exhausted version of Serena returned with Ransom to the Rio Grande Palace later that evening. *Much* later. She dragged herself to the shower and lathered her hair again and again with shampoo, wondering if she'd ever eliminate the smokey scent from her hair. After toweling off, she wrapped herself in the thick, white bathrobe she'd been unwilling to wear the first night.

Her cell phone jingled with an incoming call during her shuffling walk to the lounge area.

It was Iris.

"Hello?" Serena sank onto the sofa, wondering where Ransom was.

"I just saw the report about the fire on T.V." her friend babbled feverishly. "Please assure me you weren't in that gym, sweetie."

"How about I just skip to the part where I tell you I'm back from the hospital, and I'm fine?"

"Oh, Serena," Iris choked. "I'm the one who sent you on this job. If anything had happened to you..." Her words faded on a sob of self-recrimination.

"I appreciate your concern, but I'm fine. Really."

"You don't sound fine. You sound all scratchy and hoarse." Her friend was weeping so hard by now, it was difficult to understand her.

"My throat's a little sore from the smoke, but that's all. I promise." She leaned away from the phone to cough. "Oh, and I'm going to just throw this out there. I don't ever want to roast hot dogs or marshmallows again."

"That's alright with me!" Her friend chuckled damply. "Listen, I'm reaching for my keys right now, so I can come pick you up from the hotel. I think Mr. Keller will understand if we cut this weekend short, everything considered. I'm more than happy to issue a partial refund if he—"

"No, he doesn't want a refund," Serena assured quickly. "Yes, he would understand if I wanted to leave early." She paused to cough again. "But I don't want to."

An awkward silence settled between them.

"What do you mean, you don't want to leave?" Iris made a sound of disbelief. "Are you sure you're okay, sweetie? I've heard that smoke inhalation is no joke."

Apparently, Serena was going to have to spell things out in very plain and simple terms for her roommate. "I'm fine, and I have no intention of ditching Ransom like that. He's the kind of guy who wouldn't ask for a refund if I left early, which means he's the kind of guy worth staying for."

"Um, oka-a-ay. Do you want to tell me what's really going on here?"

Serena could hear the concern in her friend's voice and was anxious to set her mind at ease. "He and I are together now." There. That should clear things up. She twisted the gorgeous wedding ring on her finger, sad at the thought of giving it up in the morning.

"No, sweetie, you're not. Posing as Ransom Keller's wife is just a job. If you've somehow convinced yourself that it's real, then the smoke inhalation really is messing with your head."

"I'm well aware we're not actually married!" For reasons she could not explain, tears stung the backs of her eyelids. *Shoot!* Maybe the smoke inhalation *was* getting to her. "I understand I'll be taking off his ring in the morning. It's a gorgeous ring, by the way. It belonged to his mother." She gave a suspiciously damp sniffle. "You can't put a price tag on stuff like that."

"I'm so sorry, sweetie," Iris sighed. "I should have never pushed you into working one of these contracts, considering your recent break-up. It's totally understandable that the events of this weekend evoked emotions that I probably can't even begin to understand."

As she paused to take a deep breath, it dawned on Serena that her friend had totally misread the situation. *Probably something I said. Entirely the fault of my smokey brain!*

"I know he's your knight in shining armor right now," Iris continued in a soft, soothing voice, "considering how he personally carried you out of a burning building and all—"

"We were together before the fire, Iris," Serena blurted, unable to take another moment of them talking at cross purposes.

"What?"

"Ransom and I are dating."

"That's not possible," her friend declared flatly. "You've only known each other for a day."

"Oh, come on! You rent out dates for a living. Is it too much of a stretch to believe that we might've actually developed feelings for each other?"

"Absolutely!" Iris's answer was both emphatic and horrified. "That's it! I've heard enough. I'm coming to take you home, no matter what you say."

"Oh, for crying out loud," Serena exploded. "I'm sorry if I bent one of your precious rules while on the job, but I really do care for him. This isn't a joke."

Iris's voice shook as she answered. "I'm the one who broke you, so I'm the one coming to fix you." She disconnected the line.

With a rueful chuckle, Serena laid the phone on the coffee table in front of her, hating the faint scent of smoke still clinging to her curtain of hair as it fell forward.

A movement in the arched doorway leading into the room made her jolt in surprise.

Ransom paused there, folding his arms and leaning back against the frame. He looked a thousand shades of delicious in clean jeans and a t-shirt.

The knowing glint in his dark gaze instantly aroused her suspicions. "How much of my conversation with Iris did you overhear?"

He pushed away from the wall and slowly advanced on her. "Enough to make me a very happy guy."

"Really?" She scanned his features and shivered slightly. "Because you're not smiling."

"I almost lost you today." He crouched in front of her and reached for her hands. "Every time I think about it, I have trouble breathing."

"Me, too," she confessed. "The whole time we were trying to dig ourselves out of the gym, I was praying you would survive the explosion. It probably sounded more like begging." She added wryly," Or wheezing from all the smoke inhalation Iris is so worried about."

He squeezed her fingers. "Clearly, God has a plan for our lives. One that wasn't meant to end in that crusty old gym."

"Yes." The look they shared was dreamy and full of hope.

"A plan that involves us staying together, I think." He lifted the hand that bore his mother's wedding ring and kissed her fingertips. "I overheard what you said about the ring, too."

A faint moan escaped her. "Maybe you would be so kind as to forget that part of our conversation?"

"Not a chance!" He looked incredulous. "Believe me, I'm in no more of a hurry for you to take it off than you are. It would make me the happiest man on the planet if you would, instead, leave it on tomorrow morning when our contract ends. And the day after that. And all the days after that."

Her vision blurred. "But that would mean—"

"Making our fake marriage a real one, yes."

"Iris is right, you know." She caught her lower lip between her teeth. "About us only knowing each other for a day." Her better judgment was telling her to slow the pace a bit. Her heart was saying something else altogether.

"Technically, it's a day and a half," he joked. "In all seriousness, though, we can take things slow. We can be engaged for as long as you want."

"Is that what you want?" A blush rose to her cheeks as she tried to read his expression.

"No, but not because I'm trying to rush you." He lifted her hand to his mouth to kiss her fingers again. "It's because I'm so sure about how I feel about you."

"I don't want a long engagement, either, Ransom. Feel free to blame it on the smoke inhalation, but it's true." What she really wanted was for her weekend of being Mrs. Keller to never end.

"Then let's make it official." His dark gaze held hers beseechingly. "Will you marry me, Serena?"

For a moment, she was rendered speechless. All she could do was stare at him while her heart fluttered crazily beneath her ribs. A few moments ago, she'd been sad about the prospect of returning his ring, and now she was being given an even more mind-boggling option — to keep it.

"While I'm putting everything on the line here," he continued huskily, "you need to know this, too. I'm falling in love with you."

"Ransom," she choked, finally finding her voice.

"I know it's sudden, darlin', but it's not something I can blame on the smoke inhalation. It started happening the moment we met."

"At the moment, I'm too exhausted to analyze it, Ransom." She reached out to cup his cheek. "All I know is that I love you, too."

"Is that a yes?"

"It's a yes."

Then his lips were on hers, celebrating the promise they were making to each other.

DESPITE HIS CRUTCHES, Tucker kept his word about doing a better job at getting the Pack back together. Within a week, he'd planned a backyard barbecue at Ransom's home.

Serena showed up a few hours before the event, to help him get things ready for their guests. There was no need for her to arrive quite that early, but they were always looking for excuses to spend time together. She was finally wearing jeans, and she looked amazing in them. She'd paired them with a pumpkin-orange, cold-shoulder top with long, flowy sleeves that he found crazily appealing.

Less than an hour before their guests were supposed to arrive, they were hurrying back and forth across his loggia, arranging place settings on a pair of outdoor tables. It was only in the mid-seventies today, so he'd turned on the spa heater and pool warmer in case anyone wanted to soak or swim.

"Something tells me Tucker planned our next gathering here, just so he could spy on us some more," Serena declared with a chuckle.

Ransom honestly wasn't too concerned about what Tucker may or may not be up to. "Knowing him, he might just want to come check out the pool."

Her cheeks pinked. "If only! But my gut says he's still not buying our shotgun wedding story."

Well, it *was* a complete fabrication, so if Tucker was still chewing on it, it only confirmed he was clever. However, Serena didn't sound like she was looking for that kind of feedback, so he kept his thoughts to himself. He was just happy that she'd agreed to play hostess at the party, thereby keeping their ruse going. Not to mention getting a taste of married life last weekend had made him long for the real thing.

They'd applied for their wedding license a few days ago, and he'd gone to pick it up yesterday. Axel and his wife, who were sworn to eternal secrecy about all the fake bride shenanigans, had agreed to stand in as witnesses. It was just a matter of picking the perfect date and time to make it happen now.

"I don't think I'm ready to tell Tucker the truth about us, Ransom." Serena puttered over one of the fresh flower centerpieces she'd set out. "I might not ever be ready."

"Why not, darling?" He didn't see the problem "We're about to be married." For real this time.

"Because he'll never let us live it down," she wailed, straightening to face him. "These guys are like your brothers. Something tells me we're going to be seeing a lot of them in the coming days."

Laying down his stack of napkins, he moved to her side to take her in his arms. "Look at me, darling." He tipped her chin up. "Whatever you decide about this, I'll back you a hundred percent, alright?" If that meant taking the secret of their real wedding date to their graves, then so be it.

She made a face at him. "Do you think I'm being ridiculous?"

"Hey." He traced a finger down her cheek. "This is our wedding. We can talk about it if you want. We can *not* talk about it if you want. Either way, I'm happy because I'll end up married to you. It's that simple with me."

"Thanks for not making this any harder than it is." She slid her arms around his neck. They stood there together, cheek to cheek, for a sweetly poignant moment.

"Is this about your mom?" He smoothed a hand down her hair, adoring the silky feel of it.

"How'd you guess?" She burrowed closer.

"It just makes sense." He continued to hold her. "I wish they could be here, too. Both sets of parents." But they couldn't. It was bittersweet for him, as well.

Her voice was muffled against his shoulder. "I did warn you that I'm a wreck. That might not ever change."

He swiveled his head to press a trail of warm kisses across her cheek and down the side of her neck. "You're perfect for me just the way you are." He lifted his head to gaze into her beautiful eyes. "We need to set a date, darlin', because I'm ready to be 100% yours."

"About that." Her voice hitched. "There's something I need to tell you."

He tensed, hoping she wasn't about to deliver a wallop of bad news.

"StarCorp offered me the job I've been wanting."

He stared, wondering why it had taken all morning to work up the courage to tell him. "That's great news, darlin'!" He lifted her off the ground and swung her around in a circle.

A happy chuckle escaped her as she held on.

"Really great news! Wait a sec." He set her down. "Does this mean you finished your dissertation?"

A smile stretched across her face as she nodded. "They've set my official graduation date for two weeks from today. I'm finished with college. Dream job, here I come!"

Though he was thrilled for her, his mind was already leaping ahead to the details. He hoped like crazy her new job was one that would keep her in town. "Tell me more about this opportunity at Star-Corp, darlin'."

"It's a marketing research position," she informed him excitedly. "A lot of what I'll be doing is online and can be handled from home. There will be a few conferences to attend now and then, but most of those will be right here in Dallas. A few of them will be out of town."

"Are you serious?" Working from home meant his long and sometimes chaotic work schedule wouldn't keep them apart. She would be there when he walked through the door most evenings. He couldn't have been more overjoyed at the news.

"Yes, and you know what else this means?" she asked shyly.

"Lay it on me, darlin'." He was anxious to lay to rest whatever it was that was still bothering her.

"I'm ready to marry you."

There was only one proper response to a statement like that. He claimed her mouth in a very tender, very thorough kiss. "I've *been* ready," he muttered huskily against her lips.

"As badly as I wanted to marry you before now, I was worried about being a burden, if you know what I mean."

He cuddled her closer. "I thought I made it clear that money isn't going to be an issue for us." The Lord had blessed his finances. They could easily afford to be a one-income family, if it came to that.

"You did, but I want to contribute something to this marriage," she protested.

He kissed her again. "You own my heart, darlin'. What's it going to take to convince you that your love will always be enough for me?"

The clearing of a man's throat behind them had them spinning around to face their first guest.

"Am I interrupting something?" Tucker was leaning on his crutches beside the pool, not looking the least bit embarrassed about interrupting their kiss. He was so unconcerned, in fact, that Ransom had to wonder if his fiancée's suspicions about his friend were correct. Again.

"Nah, Serena and I were just setting the table." Ransom eyed Macy, who was standing next to Tucker. It appeared that his ex-girlfriend was becoming a permanent fixture in Tucker's life.

"I hope you don't mind me bringing Mace along," his friend drawled. "She's kinda useful to have around when you're on crutches."

"Meaning Tuck is shamefully milking the whole I-saved-your-life thing," she responded tartly.

Mace and Tuck, eh? Their nicknames for each other certainly lent credence to Serena's theory that a romance might be budding between the two of them. He genuinely wished them the best.

The rest of the Pack trickled in, and they were soon talking and laughing around the tables. To officially start their get-together, Tucker had to get their attention by tapping his fork against his glass.

"Someone brought to my attention that we never really got to finish our Truth Or Dare game." His announcement elicited a few groans. He and Macy exchanged a warm glance, telling Ransom exactly who'd brought that fact to his friend's attention.

"Before you take off running, let me assure you there's only one play left in the game." Tucker cocked his spiked blonde head in Ransom's direction. "Technically, our host never completed his dare, because he failed to kiss Princess."

"Whoa, there!" Ransom pushed back his chair. "You're the one who exempted me from kissing the dog, so I wouldn't get my face ripped off."

"Did I?" His friend airily waved a hand. "Between the explosion and fire, my memory is kind of hazy."

"Unbelievable," Ransom muttered. He leaned closer to Serena. She'd been right not to trust Tucker. "I say we toss him in the pool and be done with it."

Pretending he hadn't heard, Tucker raised his glass. "I propose one final dare — one I think everyone here will agree is fair. It's about that wedding none of us were invited to." He pinned Ransom with a defiant look.

Ransom shook his head in warning.

"I dare you to renew your vows in front of the Pack to include us in your nuptials the way we should have been included the first time around."

Well... Ransom shot a questioning look at his fiancée to gauge her reaction.

She started to laugh.

He felt like laughing, too, but he figured it would be more convincing to play up the moment a bit. "Don't even think about it," he growled. "We are not giving in to this goofball."

"He's never going to let it go," she pointed out in a wheedling voice.

Macy leaned forward with a sly expression. "This should be good. I'll pop the popcorn."

Tucker reached up to caress her cheek.

Ransom eyed the gestured. Yeah, there was most definitely something going on between them.

"Making a crabby guy on crutches happy would probably qualify as a public service." Serena tugged on Ransom's hand to reclaim his attention.

"Then why does it feel like feeding a monster?" he sniped, hoping he'd put up enough of a fight to make his resistance look authentic.

"Because it's Tucker," she returned in such a matter-of-fact voice that everyone laughed.

"Fine. I'll do it." He held up a hand beneath the ensuing whistles and cheers. "But just for the record, I'm only doing this because I have a smoking hot wife who I wouldn't mind marrying again and again and again."

Looking supremely happy, Serena gave a squeal of delight and launched herself into his arms.

He gazed deeply into her eyes. "I love you so much, Mrs. Keller."

She cupped his face in her hands. "I love you, too." The adoration glowing in her eyes made his heart pound.

"Aw," Matt mocked.

"Just for the record, I'm still holding out for a hot sister," Owen declared. "A twin separated at birth, a doppelgänger, whatever. I'm not overly picky." His words were greeted with another round of chuckles.

Ransom ignored them, unable to tear his gaze

away from Serena's just yet. "About that long overdue honeymoon to Venice, darlin'."

"Yes! A thousand yeses!" she cried joyfully, burying her face against his neck.

"Shoot! We'd all say yes to Venice." Owen glanced around the table. "What do y'all say about crashing their honeymoon and heading to Venice?"

Serena's head spun his way. "Absolutely not!" She looked horrified.

"I don't think this gal is going to be crashing anyone's honeymoon anytime soon," Jenn sighed, resting a hand on her blooming belly. "Something tells me our next party will be at the medical center."

Ransom decided on the spot that Venice could wait a few more weeks. He didn't want to miss the birth of the first Pack baby.

My family. He gazed around their cozy gathering, thankful for both the joys and heartaches that had strengthened their bond of brotherhood in recent days.

God was still in His Heaven, the Pack was still alive, and he was getting married — for real this time!

***

Like this book? Leave a review now!

I hope you enjoyed **The Fake Bride Rescue***!*
Keep turning for a sneak peek at

The Blind Date Rescue.
*When a painfully shy search-and-rescue surfer dodges
a blind date, then finds himself swimming to her
rescue a few minutes later...*

Much love,
Jo

SNEAK PREVIEW: THE BLIND DATE RESCUE

When a tropical storm serves up a second chance at love for a once-burnt-twice-shy kind of guy...

Champion surfer Ford Anderson is a classic shy guy. He's far more comfortable riding the next big wave than he is braving the perils of dating. So when his best friend tries to coax him into a blind date, he turns him down flat. Only minutes later, he learns that his would-be dinner date is stranded on a sinking yacht.

He wrestles with guilt as he launches a water rescue operation, knowing the lovely grad student would be safe on dry land if he'd asked her out to dinner like he was supposed to.

If he can brave the treacherous waves to reach her in time, he might just get a second chance at that blind date, after all!

Grab your copy in eBook, paperback, or Kindle Unlimited on Amazon!
The Blind Date Rescue

Complete series. Read them all!
The Plus One Rescue
The Secret Baby Rescue
The Bridesmaid Rescue
The Girl Next Door Rescue
The Secret Crush Rescue
The Bachelorette Rescue
The Rebound One Rescue
The Fake Bride Rescue
The Blind Date Rescue
The Maid by Mistake Rescue
The Unlucky Bride Rescue
The Temporary Family Rescue

Much love,
Jo

NOTE FROM JO

Guess what? There's more going on in the lives of the hunky heroes you meet in my stories.

Because...*drum roll*...I have some Bonus Content for

everyone who signs up for my mailing list. From now on, there will be a special bonus content for each new book I write, just for my subscribers. Also, you'll hear about my next new book as soon as it's out (*plus you get a free book in the meantime*). Woohoo!

As always, thank you for reading and loving my books!

JOIN CUPPA JO READERS!

If you're on Facebook, please join my group, Cuppa Jo Readers. Don't miss out on the giveaways + all the sweet and swoony cowboys!

https://www.facebook.com/groups/
CuppaJoReaders

FREE BOOK!

Don't forget to join my mailing list for new releases, freebies, special discounts, and Bonus Content. Plus, you get a FREE sweet romance book for signing up!

https://BookHip.com/JNNHTK

A scarred cowboy determined to remain single and the klutzy new ranch hand who trips up his carefully laid plans.

Asher Cassidy doesn't see himself getting hitched at a big church wedding anytime soon. Make that never. The freak fire that scarred one side of his face is a one-way ticket out of the dating game — something his interfering relatives don't seem to understand. Their endless matchmaking attempts keep him in a cranky mood.

He hires Bella Johnson as a ranch hand because

she's so desperate for money that she'll have no choice but to put up with his grumpiness, the dirtiest chores, and whatever else he chooses to assign her. By some miracle, she even agrees to pose as his fake girlfriend at an upcoming hoedown, where his family plans to dangle him in front of yet more single ladies.

Sensing her new boss's gruff exterior is hiding a heart as broken as her own, Bella works extra hard to please him...or at least not get fired for her many mistakes while tackling her new job. Her biggest mistake of all turns out to be serving as his fake girl-friend. After tripping and falling into the cocky, sarcastic cowboy a half dozen or so times, she discovers that she enjoys being in his arms a little too much.

A sweet and inspirational, small-town romance with a few Texas-sized detours into comedy!

Hope you enjoyed the sneak preview of
COWBOY CONFESSIONS #1: Mr. Not Right for Her
Available in eBook, paperback, and hard cover on Amazon + FREE in Kindle Unlimited!

Read them all!
Mr. Not Right for Her

Mr. Maybe Right for Her
Mr. Right But She Doesn't Know It
Mr. Right Again for Her

Much love,
Jo

SNEAK PREVIEW: HER BILLIONAIRE BEST FRIEND

It's not easy being the best friend of a woman he'd much rather be dating...

Titus Rand is sent to Anchorage by a top-secret organization to investigate Genesis & Sons. He goes undercover as the head of his own security firm to serve as a bodyguard — which makes his path cross again and again with Jolene Shore, a lovely nurse on their payroll. Unfortunately, his line of work leaves no time for dating.

His plan to keep his emotional distance from her falls apart when he's asked to guard the newest ward of the Maddox clan, a long-lost brother who requires constant medical attention. Though he knows it's best to keep his relationship with Nurse Jolene firmly in the friend category, it's getting harder each day to ignore what his heart wants.

Her Billionaire Best Friend
available in eBook and paperback on Amazon +
FREE in Kindle Unlimited!

Much love,
Jo

SNEAK PREVIEW: HER BILLIONAIRE BOSS

Jacey Maddox didn't bother straightening her navy pencil skirt or smoothing her hand over the sleek lines of her creamy silk blouse. She already knew she looked her best. She knew her makeup was flawless, each dash of color accentuating her sun kissed skin and classical features. She knew this, because she'd spent way too many of her twenty-five years facing the paparazzi; and after her trust fund had run dry, posing for an occasional glossy centerfold — something she wasn't entirely proud of.

Unfortunately, not one drop of that experience lent her any confidence as she mounted the cold, marble stairs of Genesis & Sons. It towered more than twenty stories over the Alaskan Gulf waters, a stalwart high-rise of white and gray stone with tinted windows, a fortress that housed one of the world's most brilliant think tanks. For generations, the sons of Genesis had ridden the cutting edge of industrial design, developing the concepts behind some of the nation's most profitable inventions, products, and manufacturing processes.

It was the one place on earth she was least welcome.

Not just because of how many of her escapades had hit the presses during her rebel teen years. Not just because she'd possessed the audacity to marry their youngest son against their wishes. Not just because she had encouraged him to pursue his dreams instead of their hallowed corporate mission — a decision that had ultimately gotten him killed. No. The biggest reason Genesis & Sons hated her was because of her last name. The one piece of herself she'd refused to give up when she'd married Easton Calcagni.

Maddox.

The name might as well have been stamped across her forehead like the mark of the beast, as she moved into the crosshairs of their first security camera. It flashed an intermittent red warning light and gave a low electronic whirring sound as it swiveled to direct its lens on her.

Her palms grew damp and her breathing quickened as she stepped into the entry foyer of her family's greatest corporate rival.

Recessed mahogany panels lined the walls above a mosaic tiled floor, and an intricately carved booth anchored the center of the room. A woman with silver hair waving past her shoulders lowered her reading glasses to dangle from a pearlized chain. "May I help you?"

Jacey's heartbeat stuttered and resumed at a much faster pace. The woman was no ordinary receptionist. Her arresting blue gaze and porcelain features had graced the tabloids for years. She was Waverly, matriarch of the Calcagni family, grandmother to the three surviving Calcagni brothers. She was the one who'd voiced the greatest protests to Easton's elopement. She'd also wept in silence throughout his interment into the family mausoleum, while Jacey had stood at the edge of their gathering, dry-eyed and numb of soul behind a lacy veil.

The funeral had taken place exactly two months earlier.

"I have a one o'clock appointment with Mr. Luca Calcagni."

Waverly's gaze narrowed to twin icy points. "Not just any appointment, Ms. Maddox. You are here for an interview, I believe?"

Time to don her boxing gloves. "Yes." She could feel the veins pulsing through her temples now. She'd prepared for a rigorous cross-examination but had not expected it to begin in the entry foyer.

"Why are you really here?"

Five simple words, yet they carried the force of a full frontal attack. Beneath the myriad of accusations shooting from Waverly's eyes, she wanted to spin on her peep-toe stiletto pumps and run. Instead, she focused on regulating her breathing. It was a fair question. Her late husband's laughing face swam before her, both taunting and encouraging, as her mind ran over all the responses she'd rehearsed. None of them seemed adequate.

"I'm here because of Easton." It was the truth stripped of every excuse. She was here to atone for her debt to the family she'd wronged.

Pain lanced through the aging woman's gaze, twisting her fine-boned features with lines. Raw fury followed. "Do you want something from us, Ms. Maddox?" Condescension infused her drawling alto.

Not what you're thinking, that's for sure. I'm no gold-digger. "Yes. Very much. I want a job at Genesis." She could never restore Easton to his family, but she would offer herself in his place. She would spend the rest of her career serving their company in whatever capacity they would permit. It was the penance she'd chosen for herself.

The muscles around Waverly's mouth tightened a few degrees more. "Why not return to DRAW Corporation? To your own family?"

She refused to drop the elder woman's gaze as she absorbed each question, knowing they were shot like bullets to shatter her resolve, to remind her how unwelcome her presence was. She'd expected no other reception from the Calcagni dynasty; some would even argue she deserved this woman's scorn. However, she'd never been easily intimidated, a trait that was at times a strength and other times a curse. "With all due respect, Mrs. Calcagni, this *is* my family now."

Waverly's lips parted as if she would protest. Something akin to fear joined the choleric emotions churning across her countenance. She clamped her lips together, while her chest rose and fell several times. "You may take a seat now." She waved a heavily be-ringed hand to indicate the lounge area to her right. Lips pursed the skin around her mouth into papery creases, as she punched a few buttons on the call panel. "Ms. Maddox has arrived." Her frigid tone transformed each word into ice picks.

Jacey expelled the two painful clumps of air her lungs had been holding prisoner in a silent, drawn-out whoosh as she eased past the reception booth. She'd survived the first round of interrogations, a small triumph that yielded her no satisfaction. She knew the worst was yet to come. Waverly Calcagni was no more than a guard dog; Luca Calcagni was the one they sent into the boxing ring to finish off their opponents.

Luca apparently saw fit to allow her to marinate in her uneasiness past their appointment time. Not a surprise. He had the upper hand today and would do everything in his power to squash her with it. A full hour cranked away on the complicated maze of copper gears and chains on the wall. There was nothing ordinary about the interior of Genesis & Sons. Even their clocks were remarkable feats of architecture.

"Ms. Maddox? Mr. Calcagni is ready to see you."

She had to remind herself to breathe as she stood. At first she could see nothing but Luca's tall silhouette in the shadowed archway leading to the inner sanctum of Genesis & Sons. Then he took a step forward into a beam of sunlight and beckoned her to follow him. She stopped breathing again but somehow forced her feet to move in his direction.

He was everything she remembered and more from their few brief encounters. Much more. Up close, he seemed taller, broader, infinitely more intimidating, and so wickedly gorgeous it made her dizzy. That her parents had labeled him and his brothers as forbidden fruit made them all the more appealing to her during her teen years. It took her fascinated brain less than five seconds to recognize Luca had lost none of his allure.

The blue-black sheen of his hair, clipped short on the sides and longer on top, lent a deceptive innocence that didn't fool her one bit. Nor did the errant lock slipping to his forehead on one side. The expensive weave of his suit and complex twists of his tie far better illustrated his famed unpredictable temperament. His movements were controlled but fluid, bringing to her mind the restless prowl of a panther as she followed him down the hall and into an eleva-tor. It shimmered with mirrored glass and recessed mahogany panels.

They rode in tense silence to the top floor.

Arrogance rolled off him from his crisply pressed white shirt, to his winking diamond and white gold cuff links, down to his designer leather shoes. In some ways, his arrogance was understandable. He guided the helm of one of the world's most profitable companies, after all. And his eyes! They were as beautiful and dangerous as the rest of him. Tawny with flecks of gold, they regarded her with open contempt as he ushered her from the elevator.

They entered a room surrounded by glass. One wall of windows overlooked the gulf waters. The other three framed varying angles of the Anchorage skyline. Gone was the old-world elegance of the first floor. This room was all Luca. A statement of power in chrome and glass. Sheer contemporary mini-malism with no frills.

"Have a seat." It was an order, not an offer. A call to battle.

It was a battle she planned to win. She didn't want to consider the alternative — slinking back to her humble apartment in defeat.

He flicked one darkly tanned hand at the pair of Chinese Chippendale chairs resting before his expansive chrome desk. The chairs were stained black like the heart of their owner. No cushions.

They were not designed for comfort, only as a place to park guests whom the CEO did not intend to linger.

She planned to change his mind on that subject before her allotted hour was up. "Thank you." Without hesitation, she took the chair on the right, making no pretense of being in the driver's seat. This was his domain. Given the chance, she planned to mold herself into the indispensable right hand to whoever in the firm he was willing to assign her. On paper, she might not look like she had much to offer, but there was a whole pack of demons driving her. An asset he wouldn't hesitate to exploit once he recognized their unique value. Or so she hoped.

To her surprise, he didn't seat himself behind his executive throne. Instead, he positioned himself between her and his desk, hiking one hip on the edge and folding his arms. It was a deliberate invasion of her personal space with all six feet two of his darkly arresting half-Hispanic features and commanding presence.

Most women would have swooned.

Jacey wasn't most women. She refused to give him the satisfaction of either fidgeting or being the first to break the silence. Silence was a powerful weapon, something she'd learned at the knees of her parents. Prepared to use whatever it took to get what she'd come for, she allowed it to stretch well past the point of politeness.

Luca finally unfolded his arms and reached for the file sitting on the edge of his desk. "I read your application and resume. It didn't take long."

According to her mental tally, the first point belonged to her. She nodded to acknowledge his insult and await the next.

He dangled her file above the trash canister beside his desk and released it. It dropped and settled with a papery flutter.

"I fail to see how singing in nightclubs the past five years qualifies you for any position at Genesis & Sons."

The attack was so predictable she wanted to smile, but didn't dare. Too much was at stake. She'd made the mistake of taunting him with a smile once before. Nine years earlier. Hopefully, he'd long forgotten the ill-advised lark.

Or not. His golden gaze fixed itself with such intensity on her mouth that her insides quaked with uneasiness. Nine years later, he'd become harder and exponentially more ruthless. She'd be wise to remember it.

"Singing is one of art's most beautiful forms," she countered softly. "According to recent studies, scientists believe it releases endorphins and oxytocin while reducing cortisol." *There.* He wasn't the only one who'd been raised in a tank swimming with intellectual minds.

The tightening of his jaw was the only indication

her answer had caught him by surprise. Luca was a man of facts and numbers. Her answer couldn't have possibly displeased him, yet his upper lip curled. "If you came to sing for me, Ms. Maddox, I'm all ears."

The smile burgeoning inside her mouth vanished. Every note of music in her had died with her husband. That part of her life was over. "We both know I did not submit my employment application in the hopes of landing a singing audition." She started to rise, a calculated risk. "If you don't have any interest in conducting the interview you agreed to, I'll just excuse my—"

"Have a seat, Ms. Maddox." Her veiled suggestion of his inability to keep his word clearly stung.

She sat.

"Remind me what other qualifications you disclosed on your application. There were so few, they seem to have slipped my mind."

Nothing slipped his mind. She would bet all the money she no longer possessed on it. "A little forgetfulness is understandable, Mr. Calcagni. You're a very busy man."

Her dig hit home. This time the clench of his jaw was more perceptible.

Now that she had his full attention, she plunged on. "My strengths are in behind-the-scenes marketing as well as personal presentations. As you are well aware, I cut my teeth on DRAW Corporation's drafting tables. I'm proficient in an exhaustive list of software programs and a whiz at compiling slides, notes, memes, video clips, animated graphics, and most types of printed materials. My family just this morning offered to return me to my former position in marketing."

"Why would they do that?"

"They hoped to crown me Vice President of Communications in the next year or two. I believe their exact words were *it's my rightful place*." As much as she tried to mask it, a hint of derision crept in her voice. There were plenty of employees on her family's staff who were far more qualified and deserving of the promotion.

His lynx eyes narrowed to slits. "You speak in the past tense, Ms. Maddox. After recalling what a flight risk you are, I presume your family withdrew their offer?"

It was a slap at her elopement with his brother. She'd figured he'd work his way around to it, eventually. "No." She deliberately bit her lower lip, testing him with another ploy that rarely failed in her dealings with men. "I turned them down."

His gaze locked on her mouth once more. Male interest flashed across his face and was gone. "Why?"

He was primed for the kill. She spread her hands and went for the money shot. "To throw myself at your complete mercy, Mr. Calcagni." The beauty of it was that the trembling in her voice wasn't faked; the request she was about to make was utterly genuine. "As your sister by marriage, I am not here to debate my qualifications or lack of them. I am begging you to give me a job. I need the income. I need to be busy. I'll take whatever position you are willing to offer so long as it allows me to come to work in this particular building." She whipped her face aside, no longer able to meet his gaze. "Here," she reiterated fiercely. "Where *he* doesn't feel as far away as he does outside these walls."

Because of the number of moments it took to compose herself, she missed his initial reaction to her words. When she tipped her face up to his once more, his expression was unreadable.

"Assuming everything you say is true, Ms. Maddox, and you're not simply up to another one of your games..." He paused, his tone indicating he thought she was guilty of the latter. "We do not currently have any job openings."

"That's not what your publicist claims, and it's certainly not what you have posted on your website." She dug through her memory to resurrect a segment of the Genesis creed. "Where innovation and vision collide. Where the world's most introspective minds are ever welcome—"

"Believe me, Ms. Maddox, I am familiar with our corporate creed. There is no need to repeat it. Especially since I have already made my decision concerning your employment."

Fear sliced through her. They were only five

minutes into her interview, and he was shutting her down. "Mr. Calcagni, I—"

He stopped her with an upraised hand. "You may start your two-week trial in the morning. Eight o'clock sharp."

He was actually offering her a job? Or, in this case, a ticket to the next round? According to her inner points tally, she hadn't yet accumulated enough to win. It didn't feel like a victory, either. She had either failed to read some of his cues, or he was better at hiding them than anyone else she'd ever encountered. She no longer had any idea where they stood with each other in their banter of words, who was winning and who was losing. It made her insides weaken to the consistency of jelly.

"Since we have no vacancies in the vice presidency category," he infused an ocean-sized dose of sarcasm into his words, "you'll be serving as my personal assistant. Like every other position on our payroll, it amounts to long hours, hard work, and no coddling. You're under no obligation to accept my offer, of course."

"I accept." She couldn't contain her smile this time. She didn't understand his game, but she'd achieved what she'd come for. Employment. No matter how humble the position. Sometimes it was best not to overthink things. "Thank you, Mr. Calcagni."

There was no answering warmth in him. "You won't be thanking me tomorrow."

"A risk I will gladly take." She rose to seal her commitment with a handshake and immediately realized her mistake.

Standing brought her nearly flush with her new boss. Close enough to catch a whiff of his aftershave — a woodsy musk with a hint of cobra slithering her way. Every organ in her body suffered a tremor beneath the full blast of his scrutiny.

When his long fingers closed over hers, her insides radiated with the same intrinsic awareness of him she'd experienced nine years ago — the day they first met.

It was a complication she hadn't counted on.

———

I hope you enjoyed this excerpt from
Her Billionaire Boss
*Available in eBook and paperback on Amazon +
FREE in Kindle Unlimited!*

Much love,
Jo

ALSO BY JO GRAFFORD

For the most up-to-date printable list of my books:

Click here

or go to:

https://www.JoGrafford.com/books

For the most up-to-date printable list of books by Jo Grafford, writing as Jovie Grace (*sweet historical romance*):

Click here

or go to:

https://www.jografford.com/joviegracebooks

ABOUT JO

Jo is an Amazon bestselling author of sweet and inspirational romance stories about faith, hope, love and family drama with a few Texas-sized detours into comedy. She also writes sweet and inspirational historical romance as Jovie Grace.

1.) Follow on Amazon!
amazon.com/author/jografford

2.) Join Cuppa Jo Readers!
https://www.facebook.com/groups/
CuppaJoReaders

3.) Follow on Bookbub!

https://www.bookbub.com/authors/jo-grafford

4.) Follow on Instagram!
https://www.instagram.com/jografford/

5.) Follow on YouTube
https://www.youtube.com/channel/
UC3R1at97Qso6BXiBIxCjQ5w

amazon.com/authors/jo-grafford

bookbub.com/authors/jo-grafford

facebook.com/jografford

instagram.com/jografford

Made in the USA
Monee, IL
20 February 2023

28292374R00098